EverGreen

ABBY FARNSWORTH

Abby Farnsworth

This is a work of fiction. Names, characters, places, and incidents are products of the author's imagination or are used fictitiously and are not to be construed as real. Any resemblance to actual events, locations, organizations, or persons, living or dead, is entirely coincidental.

World Castle Publishing, LLC
Pensacola, Florida
Copyright © Abby Farnsworth 2021
Paperback ISBN: 9781953271686
eBook ISBN: 9781953271693
First Edition World Castle Publishing, LLC, March 8, 2021
http://www.worldcastlepublishing.com
Licensing Notes
Cover: Karen Fuller
Editor: Maxine Bringenberg

ACKNOWLEDGMENTS

Most days, I relished in my writing. But on other days, it took every ounce of will within me to write even a single paragraph. Thank you to everyone who's helped me through this extraordinary process. I'd like to give a special thanks to Lynn Sommerville, who helped me finally get this book off the ground. If it weren't for her incredible editing help and advice, I would have never made it this far. And, of course, thank you to Karen Fuller, Maxine Brigenberg, and World Castle Publishing for taking a crazy chance on a young writer. You helped me achieve my dreams. In addition, I'd like to give a huge thank you to my mom. She assisted me through this process and never stopped encouraging me. Like any good mother, she believed in me when no one else did. Lastly, thank you to everyone who offered encouraging words, compliments, and smiles while I was pursuing this somewhat insane goal. Some of you will never know how much your simple words of praise meant to me on the most difficult days.

To the reader, I wish you every joy while you delve into the world of *EverGreen*. This book was written for people like you. It is my hope that you may see small parts of yourself and those close to you in Lily, Rowan, Jack, Ginger, and Giselle. Happy reading!

TABLE OF CONTENTS

Prologue

I was walking through the science wing during freshman orientation, trying to find my earth science classroom. The map they'd given me in the office was utterly useless, and the supposed tour guides were nowhere to be found. My parents were busy talking with the librarian about purchasing some new books from our family bookstore, so I was left to wander around the school by myself. Opening my school-issued agenda, I tried to see if it was any more helpful than the map. The room numbers weren't any help either, since half of the teachers didn't even bother to display them outside their rooms. My fingers flipped through the agenda, trying to figure out where the counseling office was so that I could at least ask for directions.

Finally, I found the page showing the way to the counseling office, when someone ran into me. My body tumbled backwards, landing on the floor. My books had fallen out of my bag and were all around me. Looking up, I saw a tall boy standing in front of me. A stupid, inconsiderate boy. He was probably going to laugh at me and call me clumsy, just like everyone else always did.

"I'm so sorry," he said, extending a hand to help me up.

My hand took his hand, allowing him to pull me up off the floor. His eyes traveled over me as I brushed the dust off my knee-length denim skirt. A few popular girls, one who I remembered as Athena, were laughing at me. A sigh escaped my lips, as there was no reason to get upset over the usual. My legs bent as I leaned over to pick my books up off of the floor, not wanting anyone to step on them.

"Here, let me do that," the boy said. He quickly picked my books up from the floor, dusting them off before handing them back to me.

"Um, thanks," I said, quickly putting the books back inside my backpack.

He smiled at me. "Well, it was my fault you fell over."

"Yeah, I guess." I looked over at the girls and noticed that they were still laughing. "You should probably go. You don't want to be associated with me."

He followed my gaze, looking at the girls. "Don't worry about them, they're just jealous." He smiled at me.

I laughed sarcastically. "Oh yeah, definitely jealous."

My eyes drifted to a large book sticking out of the leather messenger bag hanging off his shoulder. Leaning over, I attempted to look for the title. The book was *Mansfield Park*, by Jane Austen, my favorite author.

"You read Jane Austen!" I said excitedly.

"Doesn't everybody?" he asked jokingly.

"I wish." I brightly smiled at him.

"My name is Jack White, what's yours?" he asked.

"Lily Rhodes."

He looked over at the girls, who were whispering to each other while staring at us. He winked at me and grinned. He took my hand, brought it up to his mouth, and lightly kissed it. "Pleased to meet you," he said, obviously trying not to laugh.

I smiled at him, biting my lip to keep from laughing.

Holding my hand in his, he led me behind a pillar and put a finger over his lips, grinning widely. His hand motions indicated for me to come closer, so I did. There was a brief sensation of shock as he placed his hand on my waist, keeping me from falling as I looked back at the girls from behind the pillar. They all looked shocked, whispering to each other in urgent tones of utter amazement. Jack pulled me back behind the pillar, and we both started laughing.

Chapter 1
SENSE AND STUPIDITY

Mr. Johnson, the most boring twelfth grade English teacher at Oak Valley High School, was bashing my favorite novel, *Sense and Sensibility*.

"Marianne Dashwood is the most naïve and ridiculous character in all of Jane Austen's novels. Compared to Emma, or even Elinor, she just looks stupid," he said.

I rolled my eyes, wondering why this man had ever decided to become an English teacher. "But that's the entire point of the novel," I said. "Marianne learns from her mistakes and grows to become more mature."

The entire class, even a boy who had been sleeping with his head under his backpack, turned in my direction with annoyed expressions. Everyone knew that if Mr. Johnson's literary opinions were ever criticized, he would go on ranting for the rest of class. Mr. Johnson glared at me but quickly turned his attention to Athena Jackson. She always agreed with him, mostly to get extra credit. I watched as he engaged Athena in a detailed conversation about how some people simply didn't understand Austen's writing, and I turned my head away in frustration.

Sitting on my right side was my best friend, Jack White. He looked at me sympathetically, knowing how angry I usually was after English class.

"I know, I know," he said. "I agree with you, but that

man never will, and you just need to let it go."

I sighed and looked behind me to see that Mr. Johnson was still talking to Athena. The two had now moved on to discuss *Pride and Prejudice*. I turned back around to see that Jack was looking at me gently but also slightly amused.

"You know, Lily, this might be one of those times when I have to remind you that most people will never appreciate books the way you do. I mean, you did grow up in a bookstore," Jack said.

"Just because my parents own a bookstore does not mean I am the only person here capable of understanding the plot of a well loved and respected novel," I replied, slightly annoyed.

Jack opened his mouth to respond, but the bell rang before he could say a word, and we both headed out the door.

As Jack and I sat down together in the cafeteria, he pulled out from his backpack an apple, along with a copy of *Dracula*, his personal favorite. He quickly became absorbed in his book and left me alone to my thoughts. I started eating a bag of pretzels and looked back at Jack. His black hair fell over his silver eyes as he looked down to turn the page. He'd always loved reading, almost as much as me. That's what had drawn us to each other at first. Most people had always assumed we were more than friends, that we were secretly in love, but I'd never felt more than friendship for him. Jack and I had been best friends since our freshman year, and he was like the brother I'd never had. My parents had always been too busy with our family bookstore to ever consider having another child—they barely seemed to have time to worry about me. But Jack had always been there. He was the one constant thing in my life. He was my only true friend, but he was all that I needed.

When I arrived home from school, I opened the front door to my house and walked in. I saw a note lying on the kitchen table next to a plate holding two chicken salad sandwiches. The note read, "We won't be home until late, don't wait up for us." This was typical of my parents. The Rhodes Family Bookstore had been in my family for three generations, and my parents cared for it more than they cared for our own house. They were good people, but I sometimes felt that they cared for the store more than me.

After carrying the sandwiches upstairs, I sat on my bed. My fingertips flipped open my laptop and scrolled through my grades, which were all A's, as usual. On a whim, I decided to check the class standings. My grades were always the best, but who was in second place tended to fluctuate. My eyes were unable to look away from the screen. The strangest feeling erupted in the pit of my stomach as I tried refreshing the page, but it came back with the same result. For the past four years, I had always had the highest GPA of all three-hundred students in my class, but according to this list, I was now number two. Someone named Rowan Marx had taken my spot.

Intensely curious as to who he was, I searched my mind, trying to see if I remembered him from any of my classes. Suddenly I remembered that he was in my gym class. He was a loner, the guy who never talked to anyone. But at the same time, everyone was slightly afraid of him. He had an arrogant demeanor, the kind that seemed to say, *I could be the coolest guy in school, if I wanted to.* I'd never really paid much attention to him before, but now I was certainly interested in finding out how he'd managed to top my grades. After being number one in the class for four years, I'd gotten used to my academic status and wasn't very happy to give it up.

My hands reached for my phone. I planned to call Jack to ask him if he knew anything about who Rowan was. Beginning to dial Jack's number, I remembered that it was Thursday. Jack's family always had dinner together on Thursday nights. There wasn't much of an option—I would have to wait until tomorrow to tell him. Sighing, I went to my closet and pulled out a T-shirt and sweatpants, quickly putting them on. Then I grabbed my copies of *Sense and Sensibility* and *Wuthering Heights* from my nightstand and pulled all of my blankets on top of me. Throwing my hair up in a jumbled tangle of a messy-bun and holding a book in one hand, with a chicken salad sandwich in the other, I was prepared to stay comfortable until I could tell Jack about my newfound source of curiosity.

Chapter 2
OBSTACLE COURSE

The next morning I went to school in a good mood, but that quickly changed. It seemed like everyone was asking me if I had seen the updated class standings. I'd thought that most of them had been annoying before, but I hadn't known how much *more* annoying they could be when they were talking about something I actually cared about. I attempted to extract sympathy from Jack, but he seemed relatively unbothered — that is, until I told him who had taken my place. As soon as I told him that Rowan, a guy neither of us had ever spoken to before, was now top of the class, Jack became uncharacteristically upset. He told me he'd heard some "less than reputable things about Rowan," and that he thought it would be safer if I just forgot about it.

Jack's response to hearing Rowan's name made me even more curious, so I decided to ask for some other opinions. I asked Kayla Robinson, a girl I'd known since kindergarten, if she knew anything about Rowan. Unfortunately, the only information she could give me was that he had "dreamy eyes" and "beautiful hair." Her comments encouraged me to ask for some male opinions of Rowan since I wasn't particularly interested in hearing about his physical attributes. I asked Brian Davis if he knew Rowan, or knew anyone who did. All he managed to tell me was that he hadn't even heard of him. Brian then proceeded to "explain" to me that I shouldn't be interested in an "unpopular idiot" such as Rowan, and that if I wanted a boyfriend, he would happily oblige. I decided never to ask Brian for his opinion on anything, ever again.

I continued to ask around to see if anyone had ever actually talked to Rowan before, but it appeared that he had gone through his entire high school career without actually speaking to anybody. This was a pretty impressive feat that not even I, the bookworm of the school, had been able to accomplish. Before, I'd wanted to meet him because I was honestly impressed that his GPA had become higher than mine. But now, I was curious as to why an attractive, smart guy like him would avoid making friends. I was determined to find out more about Rowan Marx and why he was so reclusive.

My inquiries so far had been rather useless. Thankfully, I still had gym class with Rowan. Maybe I would have the chance to discover more about him, maybe even the reason that he never talked to anyone. Moving as quickly as I could, I changed clothes and was the first one out of the girls' locker room. My gaze searched the gym floor, trying to spot Rowan. Deciding that openly staring at all of the boys coming out of the locker room might look slightly strange, I decided to watch from behind the bleachers, hoping it would be more inconspicuous. After several minutes of waiting, I felt someone touch my shoulder and turned around to see who it was. Athena stood behind me, with her perfect blonde curls pulled up in a ponytail and her lips coated with an impeccable layer of dark-red lipstick. She looked at me with a sour expression on her face, which wasn't anything unusual.

"I heard you were looking for Rowan Marx," she said, her hands on her hips. "But honestly, Lily, I didn't think that even someone as socially inept as you would go so far as to spy on a boy to try to get his attention."

"I'm not trying to get his attention," I responded, rolling my eyes. "I'm just trying to...." I stopped, wondering exactly what I was trying to do.

"There's no shame in being interested in a guy, Lily. Although really, we all thought you'd been with that Jack kid for the past four years."

Suddenly there was the familiar sensation of blushing heavily. There was no way I was interested in Rowan, not in that way. No, I just wanted to know who he was.

"I'm not interested in him—" I started.

Athena held up both hands and said, "Say no more. I'll introduce you to him. It's part of my duty as captain of the cheerleading squad to help individuals of a lower social standing become more acquainted with those of us higher up on the social ladder."

There was absolutely no way I could prevent myself from sighing in exasperation. Of course I knew that there wasn't really any point in arguing with her. Athena grabbed my arm and led me over to the far wall of the gym, where Rowan appeared to be standing. Shock flooded through me—I had no idea how he'd managed to get out of the locker room without my noticing him, but it was hardly the time to worry about that now. Athena marched us both right over to where Rowan was standing and stood directly in front of him. Predictably I was already mortifyingly embarrassed, and I could feel my face becoming even more red. Rowan appeared not to notice us, or just didn't care that Athena was standing approximately two inches away from his face. He kept his eyes directed toward the ground, apparently very interested in the newly polished gym floor.

I now saw why people said he was attractive. He had golden hair, with deep brown eyes and a perfectly shaped jaw bone. His entire face was symmetrical, and he looked like a real life version of Hercules. He was really very beautiful.

After an extremely long period of awkward silence, Athena proceeded to clear her throat. Rowan raised his eyes, but instead of looking at Athena, he directed his gaze right at me. I blushed, realizing that at this point, I must look like a tomato.

"Hey, Rowan, I'm Athena, and this is my good friend Lily," she said as she quickly pulled me in for a side hug.

I didn't even bother to attempt to hide my only slightly dramatic eye roll. Rowan apparently noticed, because he was clearly suppressing a laugh.

"Lily would like to be your partner today for the obstacle course," Athena said.

I was about to interject and opened my mouth to say that this was completely not true, but Athena kicked me and shot me a death stare before I could say anything. My mouth fell wide open as I gawked at her, probably looking like an idiot.

Rowan was now openly grinning and attempting to cover his laugh with a cough. I rolled my eyes, thinking about how ridiculous this entire situation probably looked. Seemingly out of pity, Rowan agreed to be my partner. Athena, obviously exceedingly happy with herself, turned around to leave. While walking away, she simultaneously fluttered her fake eyelashes and gave me a very obvious wink with her right eye.

Rowan and I stood side by side, neither one of us

speaking. Considering how hard I had tried to find an opportunity to meet him, it was ironic that I didn't actually have anything to say to him. He turned to me and smiled warmly. "I'm guessing you didn't ask her to introduce us."

"No, I didn't," I said, more sheepishly than I'd ever said anything in my entire life. I inwardly slapped myself for being so stupid, but at the same time, wondered why I cared so much about what he thought.

He seemed to notice my inward conflict and opened his mouth to change the subject, but was interrupted by the whistle.

Mrs. Foster was our ex-military gym teacher. She seemed to think that gym class was the equivalent of boot camp and thus conducted every class with a large, shrill sounding whistle. She gave us directions and took us over to what looked like an extremely complicated, military-grade obstacle course. Every single one of the girls in the class looked absolutely horrified. The boys looked like they were about to have the time of their lives, except for one boy, who stood behind Brian, cowering in fear. Rowan stood silently by my side as we waited for our turn to race through the course. For reasons that even I didn't understand, I actually felt motivated to try to win this race. I wasn't sure where my sudden athletic enthusiasm had come from, but I suspected that it was related to all of the blushing I had done earlier.

When we reached the front of the line, I tried to prepare myself in order to have the best possible start. There was a small seed of interest blooming inside me when I saw that Rowan was standing beside me, looking rather smug, as if he already knew that he was going to win. Mrs. Foster blew the whistle, and we dashed off into the course. I made it through the bean bag toss and jump-roping areas without difficulty. Predictably, I was elated that I was only a few seconds behind Rowan, but then, unfortunately, we moved on to the hurdles. My eyes watched Rowan as he dashed over the first hurdle with obvious ease. In a dreadful lapse of judgment, I decided that if he could do it, I could too. My feet took off running as fast as I could and jumped just before I reached the hurdle. Like in some cheesy comedy, my foot caught on the top bar, and I fell face first onto the ground. A shooting pain went up through my left ankle, and I felt hot tears running down my face. This would be the story of the day. Of course, I could already hear all of the future gossip in the back of my mind. Just what I needed, to officially be the most mocked girl in school.

I felt two strong arms go underneath me, and I looked up to see Rowan holding me in his arms. My head was pounding, but I heard enough to know that Rowan was carrying me to the nurse's office. My ankle hurt so badly, but I was determined not to show it. I winced in pain and felt Rowan's arms tighten around me. He whispered that I was going to be fine and to try to relax. I decided that at this point, there wasn't much I could do except give in. I was resigned to the fact that I was injured and in the arms of a handsome man I barely knew. Exactly what I HADN'T needed today.

Chapter 3
FRACTURE

The room seemed to be spinning, and I couldn't exactly remember where I was.

"Don't worry, honey, it's only a fracture," I heard Ms. Williams, the school nurse, shout from the back of the room.

Then I remembered everything that had happened up until that point — the obstacle course, the hurdle, and Rowan. Above all else, I remembered Rowan. Ms. Williams came over and gave me a plate of crackers, which tasted like they were about ten years old. She then left to retrieve my parents from the office, who had been called right after I gracefully fell face first onto the floor. My mom hurried in with a panicked expression on her face, mumbling about how clumsiness had always run on my dad's side of the family.

Meanwhile, my dad sat in the corner of the room, examining a stack of newly released books that he was apparently considering carrying in the store. Straining to hear, I heard Ms. Williams tell my mom everything that had happened. Relief flooded through me as I heard that my ankle was only slightly fractured and not completely broken. However, I was disappointed to hear that I would be on crutches for a month. In an attempt to make the entire incident more bearable, I happily decided to consider the entire situation Athena's fault, as I wouldn't have even tried to jump the hurdle if she hadn't paired me up with Rowan.

Yes, it was all *definitely* Athena's fault.

I arrived home in a wheelchair, with my mom pushing me and my dad carrying a new pair of crutches, along with some take-out Chinese. If it had been under better circumstances, I would have been happy about all of the extra attention. My mom rolled me inside, and I scooted my way backwards up the steps for what felt like an eternity. When I finally reached the top, she helped me into bed and brought me a plate full of sesame chicken. She explained that she was sorry, but they had to go back to the store for a prearranged book signing with some local authors.

As soon as they left, I grabbed my phone, eager to tell Jack all that had happened. He picked up on the first ring, sounding very distressed.

"Lily, what happened?" he asked. "Athena was telling everyone that you fell and broke your leg!"

I rolled my eyes, thinking about the smirk that had probably been on Rowan's face as he listened to all the gossip.

"No, Jack. I only fractured my ankle. I'll be back on Monday," I said, trying to relieve the obvious anxiety in his voice.

"What happened?" he asked, sounding more suspicious than concerned.

I retold the whole story from beginning to end, leaving out the parts about Athena and how I'd met Rowan. Considering how much Jack seemed to dislike Rowan, I thought that omitting how I'd somewhat tangled myself up with him intentionally was probably best. Jack told me that he hoped I felt better, and promised to carry my backpack for me until I could walk again.

I ended the call, grateful to have such an amazing

best friend, but also confused as to why he seemed to be so against the idea of my talking to Rowan. Jack had never had a problem with any of the other guys I had talked to before, and I couldn't understand why Rowan was any different. I wasn't even interested in him in that way. Granted, I'd only been around Rowan for about fifteen minutes, but he'd seemed like a somewhat decent guy, especially since he hadn't made fun of me after I fell. Truthfully, he wasn't that bad at all. If I'd met him under different circumstances, we would probably have become fast friends. In a rather strange way, he reminded me of so many of my favorite fictional characters. There was something about him that made him a classic and mysterious man, just like Mr. Darcy. Yet he was also gentle and understanding, like Colonel Brandon.

While comparing him to all of my literary heroes, I realized something else about him, something far more interesting. The one thing he had in common with all of the different characters I loved was that he appeared to be timeless. For some reason I didn't yet understand, he didn't behave like a modern teenage boy. Somehow he seemed older, more mature. Everything about him implied that he was a complete gentleman, but was also able to laugh at a good joke. In a way that fascinated me, he also seemed to be completely free of any influence from modern culture. I admired that he was his own independent person who did what made him happy, not what other people pressured him to do. It seemed as if Rowan Marx had stepped right out of one of my books and into my life, and that's exactly the type of man I had been waiting for.

I returned to school on Monday, and as promised, Jack carried my backpack to all of my classes. We had almost every single class together, except homeroom and gym.

While dropping my backpack off in the gym before heading to his class, Jack looked around the room, surveying the area. I thought it was strange, especially since he hadn't done that in any of my other classes. After a few seconds of searching, he seemed to be satisfied and headed off to his next class. I hobbled into the gym, trying not to topple backwards with the weight of my backpack. I sat down on the bleachers and set my crutches down beside me.

Mrs. Foster walked over to me with her whistle in hand, as usual. "How are you today, Ms. Rhodes?"

"Well, my ankle hurts less than it did on Friday, but these crutches make my arms hurt worse than my ankle ever did," I said.

She clucked her tongue, as she usually did when she disapproved of something and turned her eyes toward Rowan. He was walking out of the locker room, looking more attractive in his gym clothes than I did when I tried to dress up.

"Mr. Marx," she shouted. "Would you be so kind as to keep Ms. Rhodes company for the remainder of time that she is incapable of participating in this class?"

Rowan, who was now standing right in front of me, smiled and said, "Of course. I'd love to sit with Lily."

At that, Mrs. Foster blew her whistle, which made half of the class reach to cover their ears, and directed the rest of the class towards their task for the day.

"Well," he said. "Considering the level of extreme awkwardness of our first encounter, I suggest we start over. I'm Rowan Marx."

He held out his hand, smiling at me. I took his hand sheepishly and shook it, furious with myself for being so nervous.

"I'm Lily Rhodes," I said in a voice that I hoped sounded confident. My inner self rolled her eyes, already annoyed with my obvious inability to communicate with another human. He looked down at my lap, where my hands were nervously clutching my copy of *Harry Potter and the Half-Blood Prince.*

"So, you like to read," he said. "What types of books are your favorites?"

"Oh," I said, surprised that he was interested. "I read all types of books, but I prefer classical novels."

I smiled at him, noticing how strong his arms looked and remembering how he'd picked me up so easily the day I broke my ankle.

"But the Harry Potter books will always have a special place in my heart," I said.

"Maybe I should wish to be Harry Potter then." He smiled brightly down at me through his thick, beautiful eyelashes. He reached over and untucked a piece of hair from behind my ear and placed it gently along the side of my face. "I've always preferred a more natural approach to beauty," he said.

Was he flirting with me? It was a bit of a shock. I hadn't imagined that he, an exceptionally beautiful person, would ever be interested in someone like me. We continued to sit that way for the rest of class, talking, smiling, and laughing together.

Every day I lived my life exactly as I had before, except for gym class. Every day in gym class, I sat with Rowan on the bleachers discussing all sorts of things. We talked about literature, politics, and even laughed at Athena and some of the other popular kids when they made themselves look stupid. It was quite possibly the happiest, most enjoyable time I'd ever had. Rowan seemed to become more perfect every day. Each discussion we had, I seemed to discover another one of his amazing qualities. He was patient, kind, and had a sense of humor I absolutely loved. The most spectacular part, though, was the way he looked at me. Whenever I talked, no matter what it was about, he watched me as if I was the most fascinating thing he'd ever seen. He appeared almost mesmerized with my very existence, and truthfully, I couldn't have been more happy about it. The only problem was, one day, my ankle wouldn't be fractured anymore.

Chapter 4
HOOKED

Throughout the weeks I spent getting to know Rowan, I never once mentioned him to Jack. It was almost like living two separate lives. I spent most of my classes, and time out of school, with Jack. But I spent every gym class completely focused on Rowan. It was exhausting. Rowan was becoming just as important to me as Jack, and I wished more than anything that they could be friends as well. Unfortunately, that didn't seem very likely to happen. Rowan had expressed interest in wanting to meet Jack, claiming that if I liked him, he would too. But Jack still seemed nervous every time he dropped me off at gym class, eyeing the room closely before he went to class. I wanted to ask Jack what exactly he had heard about Rowan, but I was too afraid that bringing his name up in conversation would only cause conflict.

By the end of the month, I had become accustomed to using crutches. My arms had gotten stronger, and they hardly seemed to bother me anymore. I went to gym class on my last day on crutches, excited to see Rowan. But there was one thing bothering me. I never talked to Rowan outside of gym, and after today, he might never talk to me again. Although I was a very introverted person and usually walked around with my nose stuck in a book, I got attached to certain people extremely easily. Other than Jack, Rowan was my best friend, but I was afraid that he might only see me as a way to get out of gym class. I might be nothing more than a distraction to him. The worst part was, my feelings for Rowan went far beyond friendship. At first, I thought my attraction to him might have been a crush, a result of his naturally gorgeous physical appearance. However, as I spent more time with him, I found that my feelings for him were rooted so much deeper. My feelings, my love for him was like a giant hook that became more firmly rooted in my heart every day. The truth was, I was simply afraid to lose him.

Comfortably I sat down on the bleachers as usual but was disappointed to find out that Rowan wasn't at school. Impatiently I sat there quietly for the entire class period, silently reading *City of Bones*, by Cassandra Clare. Rowan had told me it was his favorite modern novel, so I had decided to give it a try. The period seemed to go on forever. Generally, I hardly ever got bored when reading, but today seemed to be an exception.

After class, Athena walked up to me. She pulled a letter out of her purse and handed it to me. "Rowan told me to give you this. He gave it to me yesterday. I hope it's good news," she said as she walked off. She blew a kiss to some boys standing nearby as she walked away. I silently said a prayer, sincerely thanking God that I hadn't been born with a personality like Athena Jackson's.

It was almost painful to wait to read the letter until I got home. As soon as I opened the door, I dropped my things on the floor and went up to my room. After sitting down on my bed, I examined the letter. It had no address and had obviously been intended to be delivered in person. My name was neatly written in cursive on the front side of the envelope. Opening it, I carefully took out a beautiful piece of golden stationery paper.

Dear Lily,

I would love for you to join me for dinner tonight at my home, around 6 o'clock. My address is below.

28 Chestnut Street

Sincerely yours, Rowan

I carefully put the invitation back inside the envelope and sat there staring at it. This was much better than what I'd expected. I never thought he'd even give me his number, much less invite me to his house for dinner. After reading the address, I knew he only lived about fifteen minutes away. I glanced at the clock—four-sixteen. I knew from experience that if my parents weren't home by now, they probably wouldn't be home until around nine. I was sure they wouldn't mind me going, but I'd still have to walk.

In a rush, I jumped off my bed and walked to my closet, quickly opening the doors. Since today was my last day on crutches anyway, I made the executive decision that I could abandon them a few hours early. Even though I'd become pretty skilled at using crutches, I was pretty sure that taking them to dinner might ruin the mood. Since I had virtually no experience in these matters, it was a bit stressful. At eighteen, I'd been on exactly three dates, and none of them had been even a little bit formal.

Quickly I thought back to all of our conversations, trying to remember if Rowan had ever talked about clothes. The only thing I could remember him saying was that he thought skirts and dresses looked more elegant than pants. In truth, although I loved my yoga pants and leggings, I found that I almost preferred dresses and skirts. In a way different from most women, I felt powerful in a dress, so a good portion of my closet consisted of them. I opted for a dress rather than a skirt, and started pulling all of the ones I owned out of the closet.

After holding a few of them up in front of me, I decided on a dark-green maxi dress. I put the dress on and examined myself in the mirror. The dress was long enough that it just reached the floor, and was covered in tiny white flowers. It was sleeveless, so I threw on a denim jacket in case I got cold.

As usual, I decided that I wanted a relatively natural look and used a minimal amount of makeup. In a rushed manner, I moved on to my hair, taking it down from the ponytail it had been in all day. Along with my general clumsiness, I was also absolutely awful with hair appliances, but I knew how to braid better than anything. Quickly I pulled my hair back and slowly braided it in a crown across the top of my head. I fluffed my bangs and let them fall gently across my forehead. Remembering how Rowan had said that he preferred natural beauty, I pulled some small hairs out from behind my ears and lightly curled them with my fingers. Since I knew I'd be walking, I put on a pair of comfortable yet feminine black sandals. Nervously I went back to the mirror, re-examining myself. I sighed in relief. I was at least *relatively* pretty, but inwardly I knew that my dull brown hair and pale skin could never compare with Rowan's golden curls and honey complexion. In nervousness, I quickly bit my lips, hoping it would add some natural color to my face, and headed out the door.

Feeling silly for being so nervous, I anxiously walked

to his house, squeezing my handbag the entire way. My stress level increased as I reached his street and turned the corner. The entire street, composed of only ten houses, was absolutely gorgeous. I'd never actually been there before, since I didn't know anyone else who lived there. Each house was impeccably decorated. Some of them were surrounded by flowers, while others had beautiful water features or dozens of fruit trees. Each house seemed to have a considerable amount of land, and as I walked by, I sometimes saw children playing on the hills behind their houses. The neighborhood seemed magical, almost otherworldly.

I reached the end of the street where a large two-story, Tudor style house stood. It looked as though it was a hundred years old, but was so well maintained that it seemed brand new. Behind the house were dozens of trees that appeared to lead into a forest. There were rose bushes with luscious blooming flowers surrounding the entire house. I glanced at the house number, recognizing it as Rowan's. I slowly walked up the pathway to the front door and knocked.

Within seconds Rowan appeared at the door, dressed in a perfectly-fitting black suit. I inwardly slapped myself for not dressing more formally. He smiled at me, gesturing for me to come into the house. "I was hoping you would come," he said. "You look perfect."

I blushed, turning away, pretending to examine a painting on the wall. "Thank you," I said.

The table was covered in a variety of fresh-looking foods. There was a bowl of salad, a tray with uncooked vegetables, and two large pieces of baked salmon. He set the rest of the food out and sat down. I walked over to sit across from him at the large, wooden table. I glanced down, noticing that there were only two places set.

"Are your parents not eating with us?" I asked.

He looked down at his plate, focusing very hard on his silverware. "No. My mom died when I was three, and my dad passed away last year." His eyes never moved up to meet mine.

I set my silverware down, mortified with myself for asking such a stupid question. "Rowan, I'm so sorry. I know it's not an excuse, but I didn't know. I assumed that being so young, you'd have to live with someone. I'm sorry."

I anxiously squeezed my hands under the table. I kept my eyes down, so embarrassed that I didn't think I could speak.

"Lily," he said, extending his hand across the table. "You had no way of knowing. And about my age. I was eighteen before my dad died, so I was allowed to live by myself. I have no siblings, and my dad left everything to me."

I looked up at him, bringing my hand up onto the table to hold his outstretched hand.

"I didn't ask you here to talk about my parents," he said, his usual grin creeping onto his face. I smiled, glad that I hadn't ruined the dinner.

The rest of our meal went on without any other hiccups. We talked, laughed, and held hands for a good part of the evening. When it was time for me to leave, Rowan asked if he could pick me up the next day around four. I told him I'd be looking forward to it. He offered to drive me home, but I said that after having been on crutches for so long, I would enjoy the walk.

On the way home, I thought about everything that had happened that evening. But I mostly thought about how

Rowan was so different from anyone I'd ever met. There was no awkwardness when we talked, and he could make even the most boring conversation enjoyable. I couldn't imagine why Jack wouldn't like someone who was so fun to be around. I decided I would tell Jack about the dinner and my date the next day. After I told him how important Rowan was to me, not to mention how amazing he was in general, Jack would have to like him.

Chapter 5
IF ONLY LIFE WERE A NOVEL

"Lily!" I heard Jack yell frustratingly through the phone. "I can't believe you actually went to his house alone!"

"This is absolutely ridiculous," I said. "I've known Rowan for a month now, and he's a perfectly nice guy. To be completely honest with you, I haven't discovered a single thing wrong with him. I don't know why you act like he's a serial killer waiting for the first chance he gets to chop my head off. I think you're overreacting."

I was really quite proud of myself for holding my ground, and crossed my arms. Even if it didn't make me look tough, at least it would make me feel like it. I heard Jack taking heavy breaths through the phone and decided to wait for him to calm down. Jack was prone to letting his temper get the best of him. If I didn't know better, I would say that sometimes I could feel heat radiating through his palms when he got really mad. He didn't lose control like that very often, though, and it was always over something important. Well, except for the time when Brian threw a rotten tomato at the back of some freshman girl's head. Jack had gotten really mad that time, mad enough that he was about to walk across the room to punch Brian. Luckily, I'd convinced him not to. We'd had a history presentation that day, and I'd told him that I didn't want to do it by myself if he got suspended.

Finally, I heard Jack's breathing calm down, and waited

for him to start talking again. "Lily, I don't mean to fight with you, but why didn't you at least tell me you were going?"

There was clearly a genuine concern in his voice. He was really worried about me, but that didn't excuse his behavior. I knew he was trying to help me, but he was starting to make me angry. Jack was being way too controlling for a best friend. He didn't need to know every time I went to visit someone who wasn't him.

"Jack, you're really ticking me off. I didn't need your permission to visit Rowan. He's my friend, just like you are." There was no remorse, even though I could hear the emotion in my voice. Anger rose up in me, and I felt my face starting to burn. It had never ceased to annoy me that I always cried when I got mad, and I was an ugly crier too.

"I'm sorry," he said. "I didn't mean to upset you."

I could feel the sincerity behind his words. "It's okay," I whispered, feeling guilty for arguing with him.

Even if he did get mad, he was my best friend, and I shouldn't have been angry with him for trying to protect me. We said goodnight and hung up. The tears were still welling up inside me, and my nose started to run. Wonderful, I thought to myself. I grabbed a box of tissues and began blowing my nose. The tears were falling down my cheeks now, and I could feel the mascara smearing all over my face. I went into the bathroom and looked in the mirror. I was an absolute mess. My braid had come halfway undone, my makeup was in all the wrong places, and my nose was running like Niagara Falls. I washed my face, letting the hot water wash away my frustration. Gently pulling on one strand of the braid at a time, I took my hair down.

I went downstairs to grab a cup of tea and brought it

back up to my room. I sat on my bed, now dressed in sweatpants and a sweatshirt, sipping my cup of tea. After sitting quietly for several minutes, I went over to my bookshelf, looking at the selection. I had my entire Jane Austen collection sitting in the middle of my shelf, surrounded on either side by other classical novels. On the shelf above were my Harry Potter books and some other fantasy, adventure type novels. On the bottom shelf were all of my other books that didn't fit into either of those categories. I took *Sense and Sensibility*, my all time favorite, off the shelf. I also took *Pride and Prejudice*, along with *Emma*, and went back to my bed. I sat there, surrounded by my books, sipping my tea. The tears had now slowed and were gently falling down my cheeks. Thankfully, I had finally managed to get my nose to stop running. I flipped through my books, looking at all of my favorite quotes I had marked.

I finally came to my favorite one of all. "The more I know of the world, the more I am convinced that I shall never see a man whom I can really love. I require so much!" Marianne Dashwood, *Sense and Sensibility*.

Looking down at the page, I traced the words with my finger. Once I had thought those words perfectly described me, but that was before I met Rowan. Something small within me had thought that no man would ever be able to love me with the intensity that any of my favorite fictional men loved their partners. Clearly, I had been so wrong. *Everything* Rowan did made me smile. He seemed to intrinsically understand me, and I felt that I understood him with the same intensity. We were so alike, yet so different that it was impossible to describe. Every other guy that I had dated had described me as old fashioned, overly emotional, or too stuck in a book to appreciate real-life people. Rowan was different. After thinking of him, I noticed that all of my tears were gone. I was even smiling. Rowan was everything I'd ever wanted, and after tonight's dinner, it seemed that he felt the same way about me. I just wished that Jack would at least talk to Rowan, give him a chance. Jack was my best friend, and I wanted him to be friends with any guy that I dated. He just seemed so determined not to even attempt to get to know Rowan. It was so frustrating.

I grabbed a tissue to wipe my nose, noticing that it was starting to run again. Stupid boys, I thought. Part of me wished I had a female friend to talk to, but I'd never really fit in with other girls. Besides, I'd always thought that having Jack as a best friend was good enough. Jack had always been willing to listen to my boy problems before, but now he was the boy I was having trouble with. The irony was unbelievable. I threw myself back onto the bed, reaching for another tissue. My brain could only imagine how pitiful I looked. Without even looking, I took a book from my stack, not really caring which one, and ended up with *Emma*. Smiling as I opened it, I decided to start at a good part since I'd already read the book five times and knew what happened. Slowly I began reading, but before long, my mind began to wander. Somehow I couldn't help but imagine just how much easier life would be if it were a novel. All the women would be beautiful, all the men would be polite, and life would be far less stressful.

Chapter 6
THE MEADOW

My homework was done, since I'd gotten up early to do it so it would be done before Rowan picked me up at four. After changing into shorts and a T-shirt, I headed outside, even though I still had about an hour before Rowan came. Several large pots sitting on the front porch served as my garden, and I decided to work on them while I waited. I had always been extremely talented when it came to plants, somehow getting them to grow all year round, and they were always healthy. I hadn't had one plant die on me yet.

In full diligence, I was working with a couple of my orchids, trying to untangle a few of their stems, when I heard a noise behind me. Slowly I turned around to see Rowan. He was looking down at me with a strange expression on his face. In an odd way, he seemed curious, but also a little suspicious. Deciding that I wanted to know what was going on, I started to ask him what was wrong, but he began to talk before I could say anything.

"Your plants are incredible," he said. "I've never seen such impressive flowers before."

"I'm sure that's not true," I said. "You have really pretty rose bushes surrounding your entire house." I blushed, hoping he wouldn't think I was turning away his compliment.

"They don't take much work," he said, holding my hand as we walked toward the driveway.

Once we got in his car, I asked where we were going. He told me it was a surprise but promised I would like it.

We drove to his house, and he parked the car in his driveway.

"The surprise is your house?" I asked, more than a little confused.

He laughed, "No, but you'll understand when we get there."

He led me into his backyard and up into the woods. I silently thanked myself for deciding to wear waterproof, outdoor sandals. We walked through the woods, holding hands the entire way. Truthfully, I thought Rowan might have been afraid that I would fall and break something. But if that was the only way to get him to hold my hand, I'd take it. After all, he had seen my extremely poor athletic abilities before.

We reached an open spot in the woods where a thick layer of trees, shrubs, and other plants prevented us from walking any farther. A small part of me wanted to turn to Rowan to ask if maybe we were lost, but then I saw that he was moving a large rock. My feet were planted to the ground, and I was a little worried that he was going to show me an ancient tomb or a hidden corpse. He finished moving the rock and motioned for me to join him. Slowly I walked over to him, looking at what had been behind the rock. My eyes focused on a path through the trees that led into a large, beautiful meadow. Rowan motioned for me to go ahead, so I did.

It occurred to me that I had never seen a place so astoundingly beautiful as the meadow. The ground was covered in wildflowers, and there were fruit trees scattered all around. In the center of the meadow was a lake, so clear that you could see all the fish swimming around. I looked up into the trees and saw birds making nests. Looking down at the ground, I saw a swarm of butterflies flying around my legs. It was so perfect, so magical, it seemed like the Garden of Eden. Rowan came up behind me and reached for my hand.

"What do you think?" he asked.

I turned to look at him. "Oh Rowan, it's the most enchanting thing I've ever seen. Where are we?"

"It's my meadow." He smiled down at me. "My parents made it for me when I was born."

"They made this?" I asked, gesturing around at all of the wondrous things around me.

"Yeah," he said, laughing a little.

I felt something on my foot and looked down to see a baby fox. I'd never had any pets and wasn't particularly skilled with animals. But even with my limited knowledge, I was fairly sure that foxes weren't usually tame animals.

"Um, Rowan," I said, not sure of what to do.

He laughed, reaching down to pick up the baby fox. I thought of when he'd reached down to pick me up, and shivered.

"Cold?" he asked, grinning as though he knew I wasn't.

"No," I answered, blushing.

He told me to hold out my hands, and when I did, he gently handed me the baby. I moved my arms, cradling the fox like a human infant.

"All of the animals here are friendly," he said.

I started to ask how, but he put his hand behind my back and led me over to one of the apple trees.

"Close your eyes," he whispered, taking the fox out of my arms and setting it on the ground.

I closed my eyes obligingly, wondering what could be more amazing than what I'd already seen today.

"Okay, open your eyes now," he whispered, holding my hand.

I opened my eyes and saw a blanket spread out on the ground. There was a picnic basket, along with plates already piled high with fried chicken, potato salad, and apple slices.

"But how?" I asked, completely confused as to how he'd managed to make a beautiful picnic appear out of nowhere.

"Magic," he said, laughing and smiling mischievously.

He had a look in his eye that made me want to know more, but I decided not to ruin the mood. We finished the meal, which was really very good. I was surprised when Rowan told me that he'd made it himself, since my dad didn't cook. But then, remembering that Rowan lived by himself, I thought that he must have learned how to cook, or he would have starved by now.

After we ate, Rowan led me over to the lake. He took his shoes off, so I did the same. He walked into the lake, which was about waist deep, and held his hand out.

"The water is probably freezing," I said, not walking forward.

"No, it's really warm, I promise," he said, swimming toward me.

I moved toward the water and put my toes in. It felt like bathwater. It wasn't only warm, it was hot. I looked down at the fish, wondering how they weren't cooking. To my disbelief, the fish seemed perfectly happy with the water temperature. Rowan noticed the shocked expression on my face, laughed, and simply said, "Like I told you, magic."

I looked at him, feeling frustrated, wanting to know the real reason why the water was so warm. He splashed me, hot water dripping off my eyelashes and soaking my clothes. I looked back at him, shaking the water out of my hair. He was bending over, laughing hysterically. Not impressed, I splashed him back. He only laughed harder. I frowned and splashed him again. He came closer to me, and, suspecting what he was going to do, I moved away. But not surprisingly, he was faster than I and managed to pull me into the water.

Since it wasn't cold, the water really wasn't all that bad. I looked up at him, intending to say something rather snarky, but he leaned over and kissed me. The kiss was gentle and smooth. Before I had a chance to process what was happening, he pulled away. He looked worried, like I might be mad at him. I smiled, pulled him closer, and kissed him again. It lasted longer and became a deeper, more intense kiss than before. I pulled away, and we both started laughing.

He scooped me up in his arms and carried me out of the water, just like he'd done when I fractured my ankle. This time it was different. I knew and trusted him now. I gently laid my head against his shoulder, relaxing in his arms.

We got out of the water, and he softly put me down on the grass. We picked up our shoes, not wanting to get them wet, and started walking back over to the blanket. I turned around, admiring a flower I'd seen, when I noticed something strange. Whenever Rowan took a step, the plants underneath his foot instantly became larger and healthier. I watched as he took several more steps, verifying what I'd seen. After watching it happen several more times, I knew I hadn't imagined it. Rowan didn't appear to see that I'd noticed anything out of the ordinary. I decided not to mention it, concerned about what he was or what he was capable of doing.

Suddenly my thoughts went to Jack. Maybe he had been right—maybe there was something very wrong about Rowan. Maybe I'd been stupid not to listen to his advice. But as the evening went on, my fears were lessened. Rowan was still himself—charming, handsome, and kind. Maybe there was something unusual about Rowan, but that didn't mean it was a bad thing. I would find out what was different about him, but somehow I knew that whatever it was wouldn't change my feelings for him.

Rowan dropped me off at my house, but before I could escape to my room, my mom asked if he'd have dinner with us the next night. Rowan happily accepted the invitation, which before today I would have been ecstatic about. Now I had less time to investigate the possible causes for his apparent ability to make plants grow like they were the beans from "Jack and the Beanstalk."

As soon as he had left, I rushed up to my room. My mom had gone back to the store to help my dad with paperwork, so I knew I wouldn't be interrupted. Quickly I grabbed a notebook and a pen, and went to work. To all the people who had ever told me that reading fantasy books was a waste of time, boy, were they wrong now. In a hurried manner, I took stacks upon stacks of fantasy and supernatural books off my shelf. Logically I had decided that since no one actually believed this type of thing was possible in the real world, it was best to look to fictional worlds for an explanation.

I wrote down every type of otherworldly creature I could think of, marking off some of them immediately after I wrote them down. Werewolf and vampire were both quickly crossed off my list, as I had never heard of either of them being able to affect plants. Angels and demons were also quickly eliminated because I knew for a fact that he aged the same way as a human. However, I did second guess myself, going back through my old yearbooks to make sure he had aged normally. I definitely knew he wasn't a wizard, because…well, he didn't have a wand. Possibilities were getting knocked off my list very quickly, but I ended up with one idea that I thought was very promising—fae, or as most books called them, faeries. I was honestly very impressed with myself. Rowan fit many of the qualifications—beautiful, smart, and most important of all, he could influence one or more elements. In truth, I felt stupid for not having suspected it before. Looking back, it seemed obvious. He hadn't been joking earlier when he said all of those things were caused by magic. I had just been so blinded by the belief of impossibility to take him seriously. I knew it sounded absurd and that if I told my parents that my almost-official boyfriend was a faerie, they would send me to the mental hospital.

Instantly I thought of Jack. What if he knew? If he did know, how had he figured it out? Of course I understood why he wouldn't have wanted to tell me. It wouldn't have taken much thought to immediately conclude I would have said that he was crazy. I had no idea what to do. If I told Jack, and he already knew, would he still want me to stay away from Rowan? No, that wasn't an option—I knew I couldn't stay away from him.

For now, I wouldn't mention any of this to Jack. After I was positive that Rowan was a faerie, I would figure out how to tell Jack. The one thing I was sure of was that I loved Rowan, and I was pretty sure he loved me too. He'd kissed me today! Because of everything else, I'd completely forgotten about it. It had been a *really* good kiss, but it was slightly overshadowed by the fact that I now knew the guy I'd kissed was a faerie. Sighing, I flopped back onto my bed and closed my eyes. My fingers gently massaged my forehead, feeling a nasty headache coming on. In exhaustion, I laughed. The stress must have been getting to me.

After taking some medicine for my headache, I formulated my plan. I wouldn't mention Rowan or anything about faeries to Jack until I got Rowan to admit to being one. How exactly to get a confession out of Rowan? I'd figure that out later. For right now, I would closely observe Rowan, taking note of every hint of magic. My first opportunity to collect evidence would be dinner tomorrow night, and I would be prepared.

Chapter 7
DINNER PARTY

Patiently I stood in my room watching out my window for Rowan to arrive. All day I had tried to figure out ways of discreetly taking notes without anyone else noticing anything strange. After diligently preparing for my investigation, I had found several different ways to gather information, in case one of them backfired. My phone was ready to record, and all I had to do was press the button. In addition, I had my laptop already set up in another room, from an angle where it could video everything that happened in the dining room. On top of that, I had a pen in my pocket with a small notepad that I could easily conceal. If I needed to write something down, I could make up an excuse to go to the bathroom or back to the kitchen. Since I'd made dinner, no one would know whether I needed to check something or not.

Quickly I went into the bathroom, checking my hair and makeup for the last time. My outfit of choice was a light blue, empire-waist, knee length dress. The dress had small, unnoticeable pockets on each side where I would hide my pen and notepad. For my shoes, I was wearing a pair of simple black flats. Like most uncoordinated girls, I had always wished that I was capable of wearing heels, but every time I tried, I fell over. My hair was pulled up into a large bun on the top of my head, and I had done slightly more makeup than usual. I quickly adjusted a few of my hair pins, making my bun more stable.

As I heard a car pull into the driveway, I rushed back to my room to turn on the audio recording on my phone. Nervously I slipped my phone into my pocket, along with my notepad and pen, and went downstairs.

Taking a deep breath, I opened the door to see Rowan standing in front of me. He was impeccably dressed, as usual. He was wearing a pair of black dress pants and a black dress shirt. He looked *really* good. Honestly, I'd never seen someone look so wonderful in all black. He walked inside and lightly kissed me. It was just as much a wonderful kiss as the day before, but it felt different this time. Strangely, I couldn't tell if the fact that I knew he was a faerie made me nervous or excited. I led him into the dining room, where both my parents were waiting. He reached for my hand, and I let him take it, not wanting him to suspect anything.

"Mom, Dad, this is Rowan," I said.

"I know we spoke briefly yesterday, but it's so nice to really meet you," Mom said, walking over and giving Rowan a hug.

Rowan didn't seem bothered by it. "It's nice to meet you too," he said, flashing his perfectly gorgeous smile.

Evidently, my mom was transfixed by Rowan. "Robert," she said, trying to get my dad's attention. "Isn't Rowan the most handsome boy that Lily has brought home yet?"

"What, Mia?" he asked, barely looking up from his newspaper. "Oh, oh yes."

I could tell that Rowan was desperately trying not to laugh.

"We're not really official yet, Mom," I said, attempting

to sound very serious.

"Although I hope we are soon," Rowan added, putting his arm around me.

"Oh my!" my mom said, winking at me.

I had the sudden urge to roll my eyes and start banging my head against the wall. We sat down at the table with Rowan and I beside each other. My mom was sitting across from me and my dad across from Rowan. My dad had propped his newspaper up in front of his face, blocking out the rest of the world. This was what he normally did when he wasn't sure what else to do, which was most of the time. My mom was very obviously trying to mouth questions to me, and Rowan quickly caught on. I saw him smirk as she mouthed, "Have you kissed yet?" Her eyes were so wide I thought they might pop out of her head.

I looked back between the two of them, my mom excitedly waiting for an answer and Rowan smirking.

"I think I need to go check on the roast," I said, clumsily getting out of my chair and escaping to the kitchen.

I took a quick peek in the oven and then sat on a chair at the kitchen table. This was not how this was supposed to go. I was supposed to leave the room to take notes, not to escape interrogation. I checked on my laptop, making sure it was still recording. Deciding I would have to go back into dinner at some point, I returned to the dining room.

"Oh, Lily dear, we were wondering when you were going to come back. We thought you might have gotten lost," my mom said, laughing at her own joke.

Rowan continued to smirk. He made eye contact with me, making it obvious that he knew I hadn't left to check on the roast. Spectacular, I thought to myself, absolutely spectacular.

Everyone started eating the first course, which was a vegetable soup that I had made earlier that day. My dad, who still had his newspaper propped up in front of his face, began lifting spoonfuls of soup up over the top of his newspaper. I took a sip of my soup, suddenly understanding exactly why all of my favorite book characters dreaded going to dinner parties.

My mom happily engaged Rowan in a conversation about his future career as a literary critic as I continued to watch his every move. There wasn't a hint of magic in anything he did. All of his motions, though graceful and elegant, seemed completely normal. Nothing he did seemed even the slightest bit supernatural. I was starting to doubt myself. Maybe I had imagined the entire thing.

When everyone had finished the soup, I went into the kitchen to bring out the roast. As I was putting the roast on a plate, I had an idea. I could do something to force Rowan to use magic. If I put myself in danger, I might be able to compel Rowan to use his abilities to save me. It was a crazy idea, but I didn't appear to have any better options. I took a sharp knife off the counter and set it on the plate beside the roast. I picked up the dish and carried it into the hallway, where I knew that only Rowan could see me.

Mustering up all of the courage I had inside me, I twisted my ankle, doing the most convincing fake fall I could manage. As I fell, I let go of the plate, watching as the knife turned upward toward me. Closing my eyes, I thought of how stupid I had been not to consider what would happen if I was wrong about Rowan. It took all of my self control not to scream.

Suddenly, I felt something hot and soft underneath me.

Naturally, I panicked for a second, worried that I was simply feeling the floor covered in my blood. Nervously I opened my eyes and saw a beam of light filled with every color I could think of around me. The beam had stopped me from hitting the floor, while another beam appeared to have caught both the plate and the knife. As I had predicted, the beams were extending from Rowan's hand.

His face had lost all of its usual joking qualities. In fascination, I watched and saw that as he slowly lowered his hand, the beam holding me was similarly lowered to the ground. A feeling of absolute amazement flooded through me as I felt my body gently touch the floor and watched the beam of light disappear as Rowan closed his hand. The plate holding the roast landed softly on the floor, with the knife sitting perfectly beside the meat.

Quickly I stood and picked up the dish. I looked at Rowan nervously, and saw that his face was more serious and stern than I had ever seen it before. It took a lot of courage, but I maintained eye contact with Rowan as I walked into the dining room, plastering a smile on my face as I set the roast down on the table. Awkwardly I glanced back at Rowan and saw that although he was smiling, his smile didn't quite reach his eyes. My parents had been entirely oblivious. The fall had been silent, and they hadn't noticed a thing.

We ate the rest of dinner mostly in silence, listening to my mom talk about anything and everything. My dad added the occasional, "Oh, yes dear," and "mhm" whenever she asked if he agreed. Rowan was very convincing at pretending to be interested in the conversation, but I noticed that he never even touched his food.

About an hour later, Rowan stood up from the table.

He turned toward my mom and said, "Thank you for having me. Dinner was wonderful."

"Of course," she said, smiling. "I hope you can come again soon."

"I would love to," he said, smiling at her. "Lily, would you like to come with me after school tomorrow?" he asked, looking at me with an intensity so strong I thought it might knock me over.

"That sounds great," I said, looking down at my empty plate. I felt slightly guilty for forcing him to save me.

Rowan walked out of the room without so much as a backward glance. Maybe I had made him so angry that he wasn't interested in me anymore. He must want to talk to me about it tomorrow, and that's why he asked me to go with him after school.

After I helped my parents clean off the table, I went back to my room. Slowly I slipped my shoes off and went to sit on my bed. Now I knew that Rowan being a faerie wasn't going to change my feelings for him. It was clear that I loved him. Nothing was going to change that. Feeling sick, I held my head in my hands, realizing how complicated I had made this entire situation. Rowan was mad at me for putting him on the spot. He knew I had fallen on purpose. Now I risked losing him. Maybe I could apologize to him tomorrow, tell him I knew that I'd been stupid and inconsiderate. There was no way I could lose him. It was obvious that I was too attached to him to give up now. At this point, I didn't care that he was a faerie, didn't care that he wasn't human. The only thing I knew was that I wanted Rowan, all of him, and I suspected there was much more of him that I hadn't yet seen.

Chapter 8
FORCED CONFESSION

Monday seemed like the longest day of my life. Impatiently I sat through my classes barely paying attention, which was something I'd never done before. Everything the teachers had to say seemed pretty trivial compared to what was going on in my life. With a stroke of bizarre luck, I now had a supernatural, almost-boyfriend who I'd tricked into revealing his identity. On top of that, I was *positive* that he was furious with me at the moment. I was so afraid he wouldn't forgive me. Of course, I realized how wrong and unfair I had been to put him in this situation. Obviously, I should have asked him about it, confronted him face to face, rather than doing something reckless. But I couldn't change the past. Hopefully, he would give me another chance.

It was obvious that keeping his identity secret was a priority for him. It was hard for me not to worry that he might think keeping me around would risk revealing his secret to the world. The one thing I could do to make myself feel slightly better was to assume that he had been planning to tell me. He hadn't lied to me before; he had probably just been trying to figure out a way to tell me that would make me believe him. It most likely wasn't an easy thing to admit on a first date. If it had been the other way around, I'd have probably done the same thing he had. But me being me, I'd forced it out of him before he was ready. Now all I could do was ask him to give me another chance.

Gym class went by just as it had before I'd met Rowan. He never once looked at me or even glanced in my direction. I watched him the entire time, mentally pleading with him to just look my way. But he never did.

After class, I changed back into my normal clothes and walked out of the locker room looking for Rowan. He was standing by the gym doors with his backpack slung over his shoulder. His eyes were staring at the floor, a somber expression on his face. For the first time when looking at him, I didn't see beauty. I saw that powers like his could potentially do harm rather than good. What he was, was not only surrounded by magic and light, but also by a power so intense that it was impossible not to fear.

He raised his eyes to meet mine, not smiling as he usually did when he saw me, but furrowing his brow. I could feel the immense weight of the guilt of what I'd done yesterday rise up inside me. He walked over to me, keeping his eyes fixed on mine the entire way. With every step he took, I felt more guilty, more foolish for not understanding the magnitude of what I'd uncovered. I'd opened the door into an entire new world, and no matter how hard I tried, I could never shut it again. He looked down at me, his expression softening. I could see compassion and what I hoped was love in his eyes. He softly smiled — not his usual confident, gorgeous smile, but one filled with much more sadness. He took my hand and gently kissed it.

"I'm sorry for being so cold," he said, "but there's a lot we need to talk about."

Rowan drove us back to his house, and we hiked up into the meadow. The entire trip was uncomfortably silent.

Usually, I was able to be close to him without feeling the need to talk, but now I couldn't help fidgeting. Somehow, everything I did to try to distract myself only made me more nervous. Once inside the meadow, I saw that there was already a blanket with several bowls of fruit on the ground. We walked over to it and sat down opposite of each other. My stomach was churning from all of the guilt. I felt like I might be sick.

"I'm sorry," I blurted. "Rowan, I'm so sorry. I never meant to put you in the situation I did yesterday. I was only thinking of myself, not of you. I didn't think of the consequences my actions might have. It was stupid, really."

I stared at the blanket beneath me, not able to look at him. My fingers found a couple of loose strands coming off the edge of the blanket and began tugging on them. I refused to look up at his eyes, not wanting to see the anger I knew would fill them.

"I don't blame you, Lily. I blame myself," he said. "If I had been honest with you from the beginning, from the moment we became more than friends, none of it would have happened. I was planning to tell you eventually, but I wanted to protect you, to keep you safe from the parts of my world that aren't good. There are bad things in my world, Lily, things that make me want to keep you safe in this meadow forever. But what happened yesterday, it proves what I already knew about you. You're strong and determined. I couldn't hide you from the dangerous things in my world even if I wanted to, because you're not afraid of them. You're not afraid of what I am, and even more impressive is how you're not afraid to be with me. I never thought you'd believe me if I told you what I was. A fae, a faerie. I thought you'd laugh, call me crazy, maybe never talk to me again."

He reached toward me and took both of my hands in his. I sat there, stunned. He didn't blame me at all. This was a far better outcome than I had been hoping for. Logically I had assumed that I would have to earn his trust back, but that's not what he was asking for at all. All the things he'd said about me, they were wonderful. Like most people, I'd never thought of myself as brave or strong. He thought so much more of me than I thought of myself.

"The only thing I haven't figured out," he said, "is how you knew. How did you find out?"

"When we came here on Saturday, after we got out of the lake, I saw you walking. The plants grew underneath your feet," I said.

"I never even thought of that," he said. "I was so focused on you, I let my guard down."

This was getting better by the minute. I tried to keep my excitement somewhat contained, but I'd never been particularly skilled at hiding my emotions. I squeezed his hands, looking directly into his eyes.

"I want you to let your guard down around me, Rowan, I really do. I want all of you, the real you, not the mask you show to the rest of the world."

His face seemed to grow dark and even more serious. Honestly, I wasn't sure how he could manage to look so good yet so serious at the same time. He let go of my hands and rubbed his face. He put his hands in his lap, sighing and bringing his eyes back up to meet mine.

"I love you, Lily. I love you more than I've ever loved anything. I've only known you for this short time, just over a month, but every second I've been with you has been more important to me than the days I spent without you. I want to be with you, Lily. I want to have a relationship, to be your partner. But you have to know that you're the only human I've ever told about who I am. You have to know that if you were to be with me, you couldn't tell anyone, not even your parents. Faeries have existed in secret for as long as humans have walked the earth, and our secret can't be revealed now. Being with me wouldn't be the easiest option for you, Lily. You'd have to hide what I am from everyone for the rest of your life. I don't want to force you into this; it wouldn't be an easy way to live. I want to give you an out. If you're not ready for this, we can forget it ever happened."

I sat there dumbfounded. It was like I had just won the lottery, but the person who had delivered the news was apologizing about it. None of it made any sense. However, that didn't mean I wasn't happy about it. I just couldn't understand how anyone as amazing, unique, and beautiful as him would want to be with me, faerie or not.

"Rowan, I love you too, and I want to be with you. You're the only person I've ever felt really understood me. Human, faerie, it doesn't matter to me. You're the only guy I've ever been with that's loved me for me. I'm not a normal teenager. I don't dress, act, or talk like one. But you don't either. We're both so different from the rest of the world, but so similar to each other, it's incredible," I said.

Rowan opened his mouth to say something but evidently decided to kiss me instead. This kiss was different from any of the kisses we'd had before, yet it was just as amazing. There was so much more emotion. So much desperation to be loved was packed into this kiss that it overwhelmed me. It was blissful, yet urgent. Controlled, but reckless. No one word could describe the emotions flowing between the two of us in that moment. It was as if I couldn't remember when my emotions stopped and his began. They seemed to blur together into one. We, as people, seemed to mesh into a jumbled combination that was unable to be separated. Love suddenly wasn't defined by books and romance novels, as it once had been for me. Now when I thought of what love was, I thought of Rowan.

He pulled away, and I saw tears running down his cheeks. This big, strong, terrifyingly tough looking man was crying tears of joy because he had me. Nothing in the world had ever made me happier.

We got up from the blanket and decided to swim in the lake. While drying off, I thought of some questions to ask Rowan.

"Rowan," I said, sitting down next to him on the grass. "There are some practical things that it would be helpful if I knew."

"Of course. I should have thought of that earlier. It's all so normal to me that I forget it's not normal to you. All right, let's start with basic things. All faeries are born from faerie parents and age exactly the same way humans do. We eat the same foods, do the same things, and live our lives very similarly to humans. Most faeries have jobs in the human world, and live in it too. However, many fae, like myself, live in a small group of faeries. It's mainly for the purpose of community, but also provides opportunities for young fae to become acquainted and start relationships," he said, kind of sounding like he'd rehearsed his speech.

"Wait, so you're supposed to marry a fae and have a family with her? Is that like a rule you have to follow?" I asked, a little concerned.

If that was some kind of official rule, it might be a bit of a problem for us.

"No, it's nothing like that. Most faeries just choose to marry other faeries out of convenience. It's not required, it's just that most of them don't want to deal with the complications of starting a relationship with and telling a human about our world."

"So how do you keep track of everyone? Do you have a government that takes a census or something?" I asked. I could feel my inner nerd taking over the conversation, but I couldn't really stop it from happening.

He laughed. "No, we don't have anything like that. Most fae don't care any more about strangers than humans do. We stay within our own communities and mostly live private, secluded lives. We live under the same government as humans. I have a birth certificate and passport that's the same as any other person's would be. The only real difference is our abilities. Here, let me show you some examples of what I can do."

Rowan stood up and started walking toward an apple tree. I watched as he placed his hand on the tree, closing his eyes. The tree began growing, becoming taller as its branches grew thicker. All of the leaves on the tree became greener, and a few of the apples even ripened. He walked away from the tree, moving over toward a cluster of daffodils. He crouched down, cupping several of the flowers in his hands. The stems of the flowers shot upward, and new flowers started to emerge from the ground beside them. I watched, smiling. It was the most surreal thing I'd ever seen. It was fascinating to watch as he influenced and controlled the natural world around him.

I could only wonder how incredible it would be to be able to do things like that.

Rowan moved on from the flowers, walking over toward a few strawberry plants that were growing underneath another plant's leaves. They looked like they hadn't had enough sunlight and were heavily drooping. Rowan brushed away the leaves blocking the plants and positioned his palm in front of them. Beams of light, similar to the ones that had caught me yesterday, extended from his hand. The plants immediately reacted to the light and began growing. Within seconds, the blossoms from the strawberry plants transformed into bright red strawberries. Rowan picked a few and brought them over to me, sitting down beside me again. I took several berries out of his hand and ate them. They were the best strawberries I'd ever had, each one perfectly ripe and extremely juicy.

"Rowan, this is incredible! You're incredible," I said, continuing to eat the berries.

He smiled, untucking a piece of hair from behind my ear. "I suppose it is incredible. I'd never really thought about it that way before," he said. "I've spent my whole life surrounded by other faeries. I never thought having abilities was anything out of the ordinary."

He picked up a strawberry and ate it.

"Can all faeries do things like that?" I asked.

"Oh, no. Our abilities differ from faerie to faerie, but generally, they are related to the element, season, or thing that you have an affinity for. For example, I'm a summer faerie. That means that I can make plants grow, fruit ripen, and create beams of sunlight," he explained, as if it were the most normal thing in the world. If I did something like that,

I'd probably be considered some kind of superhero.

"Those all sound like wonderful things," I said, slightly envious.

"They are. But all fae are capable of using their magic for evil purposes, as well as good," he said.

I watched as he picked a piece of grass, holding it between his fingers. Squeezing it, the piece of grass shriveled up and died. I looked at him in surprise.

"So, you can burn things too?" I asked.

"Yes. The same light that I use to enhance life can also take that life away. My abilities aren't innately good or bad. It all comes down to intent and what purposes I use it for. My family, and all the other faeries I know, choose to use our talents purely for good purposes."

I smiled at him, picking up another strawberry and eating it. As cool as it would be to be able to do things like that, I wasn't sure I'd want the responsibility that came along with it. In this case, I decided it might be more of a blessing to be normal than gifted with an obligation to secrecy and responsibility.

After a few more hours in the meadow, Rowan took me home. We sat in his car for a few minutes before I went inside. He leaned over, gently running his hand through my hair. I loved it when he did that. I didn't know why, but it made me feel relaxed.

"Can I take you to dinner tomorrow?" he asked.

"Yeah, that sounds perfect," I answered.

He leaned over farther, keeping his hand in my hair while kissing me. He grinned, seemingly back to his charming self.

"I love you, Lily Rhodes," he whispered, his forehead

still pressed against mine.

"I love you too, Rowan Marx," I said, leaning in for another perfect kiss.

Chapter 9
MAY I HAVE THIS DANCE?

I didn't know if we were going somewhere formal for dinner or just casual, so I'd chosen an outfit that was somewhere in the middle. I'd decided to wear a black flared mini-skirt along with a pink V-necked blouse. My shoes were a pair of pink flats that had small roses embroidered on them. They were probably my favorite pair of shoes, but I hardly ever wore them. They never seemed to go with what I was wearing. My hair was pulled back in a tight French braid, and I'd lightly curled my bangs.

I was standing on the front porch waiting for Rowan to pick me up when I noticed that a few of my mint plants were starting to droop. I'd been spending so much time with Rowan that I had been neglecting my garden. After going inside to get some water, I slowly poured it at the base of the plants. I had almost emptied the container when I felt two strong arms reach around from behind me and grab my hands. Rowan bent down, softly kissing my neck.

"Hey," he said, his arms still tightly around me.

"You surprised me," I said. "I didn't know you were here."

He leaned over and kissed me again. "Do you know now?" Rowan asked, grinning.

I rolled my eyes, putting my hands on my hips. He looked down at my mint plants and seemed to notice that one of them was still drooping. He reached down and touched the base of the plant. Within seconds the plant was standing taller than all of the others around it.

"And I thought I was good at gardening," I mumbled.

"You are," he said. "Just not as good as me."

I jokingly punched his arm, frowning. He laughed, grabbed my hand, and led me toward his car.

We drove to a small, family-owned restaurant. I'd been there once before with my parents. They mostly served Italian food, but they also had some other options. Rowan came around to my side of the car and helped me out. We held hands as we walked to the front door.

"I wonder why there are only two other cars in the parking lot," I said, looking around at the vacant parking spaces.

"That would be because I reserved the whole restaurant from six to eight," Rowan said, smirking.

I looked at him, my mouth hanging open in what I assumed was a very unattractive way. I quickly closed it, wondering why I did those types of things. He grinned, picking my hand up and kissing it.

"My lady," he said, holding the door open and motioning for me to go inside.

I walked in to see that all of the lights were turned off. The room was lit by dozens of candles, but only one table was set. It was in the middle of the room and already had two plates on it piled high with pasta and breadsticks. There was a bundle of white lilies tied with a ribbon set on one of the chairs.

"Rowan, you really didn't have to do this," I said.

"Ah, but I wanted to. Faeries are very traditional, and

our ladies always have the best. My father left me with lots of money and investments that bring in more every month. He told me that he didn't care what I did with any of it, as long as half of it was spent on the woman I loved."

There was no way I could thank him, so I kissed him lightly on the cheek instead. We sat down and started on our pasta. I had a spinach ravioli with a white garlic sauce. It was so good that I ate every single bite. I tried to eat relatively neatly, but the sauce made it very difficult. Rowan had spaghetti noodles covered in olive oil and sprinkled with several different types of cheese.

We had finished eating when I noticed Rowan had placed a small box on the table. He reached over and took my hand in his. He picked up the box and gently placed it in my hand. I opened the box and saw a small diamond pendant shaped like a flower. The pendant was attached to a silver chain that by itself looked as if it had cost a fortune.

"Do you like it?" Rowan asked.

"Rowan, it's gorgeous, but it looks so expensive," I said.

I looked over at him worriedly. He shouldn't have spent that much money on me, not yet at least.

"All that matters is that you like it," Rowan said.

"I love it," I replied.

"Will you go to prom with me?" he asked.

"Of course," I said, squeezing his hand.

Rowan stood up and walked over to me. He carefully took the necklace out of the box and hung it around my neck. The chain was long enough that the pendant hung right below my collar bone. I reached up, tracing the outline of the pendant with my hand. Rowan leaned over and softly kissed the top of my head.

"There's just one problem," he said. "I can't dance any better than a baby elephant on stilts."

I laughed, but then realized that Rowan was stone faced and absolutely serious.

"It's okay, I'll teach you. Despite the fact that my athletic abilities are completely lacking, I can dance very well. When I started reading Jane Austen, I forced my parents to teach me. That was when I was twelve, so I've got some experience," I said.

I walked over to him and arranged his hands, one on my waist and the other holding my hand. I started dancing and pulled him along with me. It took about ten minutes, but he eventually got the hang of it. We danced for a while longer and soon started doing twirls and spinning around the room. I'd never danced with anyone other than my dad and Jack. I'd always dreamed of dancing with someone I loved. Someone I loved in a romantic way, that is. By the end of our dance, Rowan seemed to be enjoying himself as much as I was. But we both began to tire and sat back down to rest. Rowan pulled his chair over next to mine. He put his arm around my back, and I rested my head on my shoulder.

"That was a lot more fun than I'd expected," he said. "I usually work out to burn energy, but I might have to start dancing instead."

I laughed, moving my head to look up at him.

"I would be a very willing dance partner, but it's rude to ask a lady for more than two dances in a row. You might have to find someone else to dance with, although I'm not sure I like the thought of you dancing with someone else."

"Why would I dance with anyone else when I already

have the most mesmerizing woman in the world right here with me?" Rowan asked.

He leaned over and kissed me. It was the kind of kiss that wiped away any uncertainties I ever had about not being enough for him.

We sat in Rowan's car in my driveway for a while after we got back to my house. I knew I had to tell him my suspicions about Jack, not that I was looking forward to it. I had no interest in ruining the mood.

"Rowan," I said, "I think Jack knows, or at least suspects, that you're not human. It would explain why he doesn't trust you."

"Maybe if I met him, had a chance to talk to him for a while, I could convince him that I'm normal. Without proof, most humans give up on any suspicions they have about us."

I sighed, not particularly liking the idea of intentionally deceiving my best friend. I looked down at the ground, not wanting to meet Rowan's eyes.

"Lily, you know we can't tell him. That was part of the deal for us being together; none of your friends or family can know what I am," he said.

"I know," I said, still not exactly thrilled with the idea of lying.

"But I promise, if you can get him to talk to me, I'll try to be friends with him," he said, his voice sounding sympathetic.

"All right, I'll talk with him tomorrow. If I tell him it's important to me, I might be able to get him to change his mind."

He smiled, reaching over to hold my hand. "Speaking of friends, I'm going to take you to meet mine," he said.

"Wait, your faerie friends? Is that allowed?" I asked.

He laughed, smiling his addictive smile that I could never get enough of. "Of course it's allowed. My cousins have been dying to meet you."

"Your cousins?" I asked. "I didn't even know you had cousins."

"My mom's sister has twin daughters, Ginger and Giselle. They're nineteen," he said.

"You know I don't fit in well with other girls," I said skeptically.

He grinned with the familiar glint of mischief showing in his eyes. "Oh, don't worry," he said. "They'll do all the talking. Those two could talk a brick wall into wearing a ball gown."

Chapter 10
PROM?

I sat down at lunch, finally prepared to talk to Jack about Rowan. Jack had to know that Rowan was an important part of my life. If he really cared about my happiness, he would accept that. I was determined to convince Jack to at least give Rowan a chance. Jack sat down beside me, pulling out his chemistry notebook.

"Hey, can we talk?" I asked.

"Yeah, of course," he said. "What's up?"

I took a deep breath, preparing myself for his inevitable anger. "I've been seeing Rowan regularly, and I'm planning to continue seeing him."

Jack's smile instantly faded with the mention of Rowan's name. "So you're like a thing now? You're official?"

I noticed his hands were clenched into tight fists. He was letting his temper get out of control again.

"Yes. I wanted to tell you before, but I was afraid you'd be mad." I said. I reached down, touching his hands. They were hot, really hot. "Are you okay?"

"Fine," he said, pulling his hands away from me.

"Jack, please," I said, pleading with him. "I want the two of you to at least try to get along. Rowan wants to meet you, to talk with you. Couldn't you at least try, for me?"

"Lily, I already told you. I don't trust him. A few of the cheerleaders even said that he cheated on his ex, and that's why he hasn't had a girlfriend since last year. I don't want you to get hurt."

I sat still, taking a moment to process what Jack had said. I'd asked Rowan about his past relationships, and he'd told me that he'd only dated one other girl. She was a faerie and had graduated last year. He had said that she liked him far more than he had ever liked her and that the relationship had only lasted a couple of months. I trusted him way more than I trusted a bunch of girls who just liked to stir up drama.

"Jack, you know what those girls are like. They make up stories about people just to have something other than their hair and nails to talk about. I trust Rowan. He's a good guy, and he'd never hurt a girl like that."

Jack stared at me. I could see the anger behind his eyes. It was way more intense than I had expected.

"So you don't believe me? Lily, I've been your best friend for four years! Why are you taking his side? You barely know this guy! Look, if there's some kind of problem we need to talk about—a drug problem, an addiction…. Does he have something on you?" he asked.

My jaw dropped. He was asking me if Rowan was forcing me to be with him. And he was accusing me, the girl who was considered to be the smartest in the school, of being on drugs! Now my anger was definitely stronger than his. I wasn't going to let him say those types of things about me, or Rowan.

"I tell you that I'm going out with a guy that I like, and you accuse me of being on drugs?!" I yelled.

He flinched, looking away like a puppy who had been scolded. But I didn't care. He'd gone too far this time. He reached over toward me, trying to hold my hand. I pulled away, turning my back toward him.

"Lily, I'm sorry," he said, looking as if he wanted to say more.

"Don't," I said, holding up my hand.

I felt something touch my arm and looked down to see a rose with a card tied to it. I untied the ribbon that had been holding the two together and opened the card.

Lily,
Prom?
Jack

I closed the card, looking back over at Jack. He was standing up with his backpack on.

"I was going to give it to you earlier," he said, "but I assume you're going with him now. I understand if you're too mad to talk to me for a while. Call me when you want to talk."

He looked genuinely sorry, but I wasn't ready to forgive him yet. He was being overprotective and controlling. Jack had always had a temper, but he'd never tried to control me before I'd started talking to Rowan. I looked back down at the rose in my lap, gently picking it up. Part of me felt guilty. But another part of me told myself that if I didn't hold my ground, Jack would never understand how important Rowan was to me. I'd give him time. After a few days, neither of us would be angry anymore, and maybe he'd agree to give Rowan a chance.

Frustrated, I went home to an empty house. There was some soup on the stove and a plate of cookies on the counter, but I wasn't hungry. With my mind spinning, I went up to my room and put my things down on the floor. Hurriedly I found a jar, filled it up with water, and put the rose that Jack had given me in it. After looking at it for several moments, I placed the jar on my nightstand and lay down on my bed. After a few minutes, I noticed the vase of flowers near my window that held the lilies Rowan had given me last night. Without much thought, I went to the window and exchanged the lilies for the rose, putting the lilies beside my bed. Somehow, it felt better this way.

A few months ago, my life had been completely drama free. The only romantic problems I used to have to worry about were either the ones in my books or the fact that I had no romantic problems to worry about. Now I had a perfect boyfriend. Faerie or not, he was exactly what I had pictured as a little girl when I'd thought of Prince Charming. But I couldn't seem to get my best friend to even speak to him. Jack had heard some rumors about Rowan, and if I didn't know Rowan, I might have believed them too. However, I did know Rowan, and everything in his behavior indicated that he would never intentionally hurt a girl. He was respectful in every way, and I knew that he could never bring himself to hurt another person so deeply as to cheat on them. Plus, the source from which the rumors had stemmed wasn't exactly who I would call reliable. Jack should have believed me over some cheerleaders that we barely knew. He was treating me like I was some naïve little girl who didn't know how to handle her own love life.

My phone started to ring, and I reached over to look at it. Jack was calling me. I was definitely not ready to talk to him again yet. Quickly I pressed "deny," fully aware that he could tell I'd denied the call. Well, I never said I wasn't a little dramatic.

The rest of the week passed rather uneventfully. It hurt me to keep denying Jack's calls, but I knew a conversation would only lead to a fight. Honestly, I was still mad. He'd accused me of being on drugs and claimed that my boyfriend was a manipulative cheater. Maybe I was crazy, but I thought this warranted the silent treatment for at least a few more days. He needed to finally get the idea that Rowan was a permanent part of my life and wasn't going anywhere. If not, I didn't know what I would do.

Chapter 11
MORE LIKE FAMILY

As promised, Rowan had arranged for me to meet all of his faerie friends and family. Although he was only biologically related to his aunt, uncle, and two cousins, he told me that the rest of them were just as important to him. They had arranged a welcoming party for me so I could meet everyone at the same time. I tried to dress well. I wore a lacy green sheath dress, the necklace Rowan had given me, and black flats. My hair was pulled back into a low, braided-bun, and I'd let my bangs fall naturally across my forehead. I remembered what Rowan had told me about his cousins being excessively outgoing. It made me nervous, considering that most of my friendships were fictional characters, and I didn't have many social skills. I generally tried to avoid people, but there were some situations, like this one, where that wasn't possible.

Rowan picked me up and drove us to his cousin's house where the party was being held. The house was a white, ranch style with a large front porch and many windows. It sat directly to the left of Rowan's house. I didn't know if I'd want to live surrounded by people I knew, but it didn't seem to bother him.

Rowan and I walked up to the front door, and I held on tightly to his arm. I could tell that the opinions of Rowan's family were very important to him, and I desperately wanted to impress them. Rowan gave me a reassuring smile, wrapping his arm around my back. He knocked lightly on the door, and within what seemed to be less than a second, it opened. A middle-aged woman with waist-length frizzy, red hair and wearing a floor-length maxi dress stood before us. She smiled warmly at me, then kissed Rowan on the cheek. She quickly ushered us inside, closing the door behind us.

"Lily, this is my aunt, Marie Jones," he said.

"It's so lovely to meet you, dear." She pulled me in for a quick hug and kissed my cheek. "Everyone else is waiting in the living room," she said. "They're just so anxious to meet you. I didn't want you to be overwhelmed, though, so I told them to wait until we at least got you in the house." She smiled.

Rowan squeezed my hand, obviously trying to calm my nerves. Marie led us through a hallway and into a large room filled with comfortable looking chairs and couches, most of which were occupied. There was a table piled high with cookies, cakes, and other snacks. There was also a separate table covered in a variety of fruits, vegetables, and cheeses. I realized everyone was staring at me and tried to think of something to say.

"Uh, hi, I'm Lily," was all I managed to get out.

I saw a flash of red, and suddenly two pairs of arms were around me. It felt as if I was being squeezed so tightly that I might be cut in half. I looked at Rowan, who was grinning.

About as quickly as the two sets of arms had been wrapped around me, they disappeared. Suddenly I could breathe again. Standing in front of me were two girls who looked almost exactly like Marie. The only difference was that their hair was only long enough that it fell just below their shoulders rather than down to their waist. Their faces were covered in freckles, and they had piercing blue eyes.

"Hi, I'm Ginger, and—"

"I'm Giselle," the other cut in.

"We're Rowan's cousins," Ginger added, beaming at me.

"We were so, so, so excited to meet you." Giselle was bouncing like a kangaroo.

"But we know you have to meet everyone else," Ginger said, "so we'll fill you in on all of the shopping plans later."

They darted off towards the cookies and left Rowan and me standing alone.

"Shopping plans?" I asked, not understanding what was going on.

"They've already made plans to take you shopping. I tried to get them to wait until they met you, but they obviously didn't listen," Rowan whispered in my ear.

I turned back around to see an older couple standing in front of us.

"Hello, sweetie. I'm Charlotte Wood, and this is my husband, Will. I'm so glad Rowan found you. He's been dreadfully lonely since his father passed last year. Cancer, awful disease. Anyway, he's been so much happier since he met you." Both Will and Charlotte smiled kindly as they walked away.

Another couple, far younger than the Woods, took their place. Behind them stood a small girl. She had long brown hair, very similar to mine, and appeared to be around three years old. She peeked out from behind the woman's leg, staring up at me. If I could have gotten away with it, I probably would have hidden behind Rowan the same way. Sadly, I didn't have that option.

"Hi! It's great to meet you. I'm Clay Marshall, and this is my wife, Tiffany." He gestured to his wife, who had reached down to pick up the little girl.

"This is our daughter, Lizzy," Tiffany added, smiling proudly.

Lizzy grinned at me. She raised her palm toward me and produced a small gust of wind that smelled of pumpkins and dried leaves.

"Lizzy is a fall faerie," Rowan explained.

I smiled at Lizzy, and she grinned back at me.

Clay whispered something I didn't hear to Rowan, causing them both to laugh. After a few minutes of talking, everyone else seemed to be heading into the backyard, so we followed.

Outside, there were dozens of chairs set up, as well as tables full of food and an unlit fire pit. I watched as Ginger and Giselle put their hands together and threw a ball of fire into the fire pit. I assumed they must be fire faeries.

As we walked around, Rowan filled me in on who everyone else was. Victoria and Thomas Smith were a middle-aged couple with three sons: Colton, Carson, and Cameron. Colton and Carson were both in middle school, while Cameron had just started high school this year. I noticed that Carson looked very similar to Rowan, with golden hair and tan skin. Rowan explained that this was because they were both summer faeries.

Anthony Lincoln was a much older man who looked to be around seventy-five. Despite his age, he was throwing a football with the Smith boys and seemed to have more energy than any of them.

Eleanor and Daniel Norris were a young couple in their early twenties. They both had caramel colored skin and curly black hair. Eleanor was obviously pregnant, as her bump protruded from her flower-covered blouse.

Eva and Issac Crane, who Rowan told me were Eleanor's parents, appeared to be about the same age as the Woods but much more lively. They were sitting beside the Woods playing a card game. From the look of the situation, Issac was playing for both himself and Will. It probably would have been a very amusing game to watch.

Caroline Welsh, similarly to Carson, very closely resembled Rowan. Although she seemed to be in her early fifties, I thought she might have been the most beautiful woman I'd ever seen. She had long, blonde curls that tumbled down her back, reaching her waist. Her skin was a honey colored tan, and she was tall, as well as extremely thin. From what I could tell, all summer faeries looked like angels. Rowan later told me that Caroline not only looked like an angel, but also had the heart of one. Everyone there seemed completely gorgeous, with impeccable hair. Honestly, I was more than a little jealous. I wondered if I were a faerie, maybe I'd look like an angel too.

My eyes looked around at the happy scene. Everyone seemed to be enjoying themselves. There was no tension between anyone, except for two people sitting in the corner. Interestingly I hadn't noticed them before, but now that I had, I couldn't look away. They were such a stark contrast from everyone else. They appeared to be a father and daughter duo. The girl had long, silky black hair and skin that was even paler than my own. That in itself was surprising. In all my life,

I had rarely come across anyone whose skin was lighter than mine. The difference was that hers was utterly flawless. She looked as though she were a perfect porcelain statue, with curves in all the right places. It didn't take much to realize that I certainly didn't have those. She was wearing a skin-tight black dress that barely qualified as mid-thigh. Personally, I wouldn't have ever dreamed of wearing anything that short, maybe because I wouldn't have looked half as good as she did. Her heels were outrageously tall, but she was able to walk in them like they were the most comfortable shoes in the world. It was impossible not to think how clumsy I would look in comparison. Suddenly I realized who she must have been. Rowan's ex-girlfriend, Delilah Banks. He had told me that she was a lightning fairy and that she was nineteen. What he *hadn't* told me was that she looked like a supermodel.

Standing beside her was a man I presumed to be her father. Her father had the same dark hair and light skin as she did, but he looked much tougher. Honestly, he was terrifying looking, sort of like a bouncer. The tattoos covering his arms didn't help shake the image either. Her father was talking to Forest, Rowan's uncle. Both men had large, sturdy builds. However, Forest's demeanor looked protective, while the other man's looked aggressive.

Delilah's eyes locked on mine and she raised one perfectly groomed brow quizzically. I watched as she looked me up and down, examining me. She smirked, but with a much crueler undertone than Rowan ever had. I had always thought Athena was judgmental, but the looks she gave had nothing on Delilah's. In a confident manner, she put her hands on her hips, looked back at me, and rolled her eyes. I thought back to my argument with Jack earlier that week;

there was no way Rowan would have ever cheated on her. To be honest, if I were Rowan, the looks she gave would have made me afraid to break up with her. I would have worried that she would claw me to death in my sleep with her pointy, fake nails.

Rowan touched my shoulder. "Are you all right? You look like someone's just threatened to murder you — or worse, burn all your books and make you watch."

I knew he was trying to make me laugh, to make me feel better. But I couldn't help but feel slightly deceived. It wasn't even a fair game if I didn't know that my competition had dozens of tools to stab me with, literally and figuratively.

"Why didn't you tell me?" I demanded.

"Tell you what?" He took a step back, obviously surprised by my aggressive tone.

"That your ex is like, Aphrodite incarnate!" I whispered in a frustrated tone, throwing my hands up in the air.

He laughed, exasperated. "Delilah may be physically beautiful, but her personality is like ice, and her heart is just as cold." He reached down and squeezed my hand. "There's no one I want except you."

Somewhere inside me, I knew it was childish to be jealous, but I really couldn't help it. As much as I could, I tried to ignore my worries, pushing them to the back of my mind. If Rowan had loved Delilah instead of me, he would have been with her. My hands moved up to run through his hair, once again admiring its texture. He grinned at me, playfully shaking his head back and forth. Behind me, I heard someone clear their throat and turned around. Delilah was standing in front of us, her hands on her hips. She batted her lashes at Rowan, reaching up to touch the choker around her neck. I felt my hand drift up toward the necklace Rowan had given me. In that moment, I needed all the comfort I could get.

"So, Rowan, this is the girl we've been hearing all about." Delilah ran her hand through her hair, flipping it over her shoulder. "She's a little thin, don't you think? Doesn't look like she has any curves."

I stared at her, both shocked and disgusted. I'd never heard someone be so openly obnoxious.

Rowan's mouth was pressed into a thin line. "Seriously, Delilah? That wasn't really necessary."

He spoke as if he were scolding a child, and she looked a little hurt by his accusing tone. She obviously wasn't too torn up about it, though, because she quickly recovered.

Delilah smiled innocently. "She's just a distraction. You'll be fascinated by your little human girlfriend for a while. But in the end, you'll run back to me. We're made for each other."

She reached over to touch Rowan's face. He stepped back, moving away from her. I grabbed her wrist, inches away from his face.

"Oh, so she's a feisty little thing, isn't she?" Delilah laughed.

I was about to pull her hand down and let go when she shocked me. I felt as if my entire arm was being electrocuted. The pain was indescribable; I'd never felt anything like it. My hand reflexively let go of her wrist, and the pain stopped. I pulled my arm in close to me, cradling it. Rowan stepped in front of me, looking furious.

"Don't worry," Delilah said. "A little lightning never hurt anyone."

She grinned at me, winked at Rowan, and walked

away. I shook my arm, the shock wearing off.

"Lily, I'm so sorry! Are you okay?" Rowan touched my arm. His eyes held so much guilt that I could barely look at him.

"It's not your fault." I cupped his face in my hands, quickly kissing him. "Talk about a psychotic ex," I muttered.

Rowan laughed nervously, smiling at me.

We finished eating, and some people started saying their goodbyes. Both the Smiths and Marshals left, wanting to put their kids to bed. Daniel and Eleanor Norris soon followed, saying they were trying to get all the rest they could before the baby arrived. Everyone else had their individual reasons for leaving, and soon it was only me, Rowan, and the Jones family.

Before I knew what was happening, Ginger and Giselle whisked me away up into their bedroom. I had never seen so much pink in my life. I imagined that if a five-year-old girl could have designed her own bedroom, it would look something like this. The walls, ceiling, and floor were all pink. There were two twin beds in the center of the room, each covered in sparkly pink blankets and pillows. And there was glitter everywhere. Glitter, glitter, and more glitter. Although some people might have considered me a hopeless romantic, I was not "girly." Sparkles and glitter were not my thing. The girls flung themselves down onto beanbags, which were pink, naturally. Not knowing what else to do, I awkwardly sat down on a fluffy pink chair.

"Did Rowan tell you?" Giselle asked.

"Tell me what?" I nervously played with the hem of my dress, not really sure what to make of the two of them. I was convinced they had more combined energy than a class full of five-year-olds.

"About our shopping trip!" Giselle squealed.

I was positive I'd never heard a more high pitched sound in my life. It made me want to cover my ears and run for the door.

"It's next Saturday," Ginger added.

"Oh, right. I forgot," I said.

"I could never forget about shopping," Giselle sighed, squeezing a neon pink elephant.

If the elephant had been alive, I was fairly sure she would have strangled it.

"What exactly are we shopping for?" I asked, nervously.

"A prom dress for you, of course! We've been so excited to meet you! We tried to convince Rowan to let us meet you earlier, but he said you were shy." Ginger bounced in her beanbag.

"Wonder why," I mumbled under my breath.

"We saw what happened with Delilah earlier. She's meaner than a snake!" Giselle stuck her tongue out.

I resisted the urge to roll my eyes. As if I hadn't noticed her evil tendencies. After all, I was the one she'd attempted to electrocute. She'd almost been successful, too.

"I always knew she was a witch!" Ginger made an ugly face.

I laughed. "Witch, I like that."

They smiled at me and burst into giggle attacks. Maybe these two weren't all that bad.

After Rowan dropped me off at my house, I went into the bathroom and took a bubble bath. It felt heavenly to let my hair float around me in the water and close my eyes. My nose inhaled as I smelled the essential oils flowing out of my diffuser. Finally, at peace, I relaxed my shoulders, letting myself float in the water. Unable to completely calm my mind, I thought back through the events of the day, trying to process everything that had happened. Most of Rowan's friends were kind, friendly, and inviting. They were far more attentive and neighborly than most humans. His family, however strange they might be, really weren't that bad either. It was clear that Marie was more of a mother to Rowan than an aunt. He loved her just as much as he would have loved his real mother if she were alive. Ginger and Giselle were unique, but they were also a lot of fun. Truthfully, I had enjoyed being around all of them. It was odd that I felt like I fit in more with them than I did with humans. Well, all of them except Delilah.

If there was ever a real life wicked witch, it would have been her. I would have been perfectly content if she were to disappear into oblivion, never to be seen or heard from again. The thought made me smile, but I doubted that was going to happen. Thankfully, I knew that Rowan loved me and was fully committed to making our relationship work. If I hadn't been so sure of that, I might have been terrified. Delilah was annoying, but she would eventually figure out that I wasn't going anywhere. I'd heard of people having crazy possessive exes before. I'd just never heard of one who shot lightning out of her hands.

Chapter 12
Jealousy: A Poison To The Soul

  I went back to school on Monday, still angry with Jack. He'd called endless times since our fight, no doubt to apologize. Honestly, I just wasn't ready to forgive him yet. When I thought about it, I was fairly sure he hadn't changed his mind about Rowan, and until he did, we didn't have anything to talk about. There was no way I was giving up on Rowan, and I shouldn't have had to. It was Jack's job as my best friend to stay by my side, not abandon me in a split second just because he didn't like the guy I was dating. He didn't even have a good reason to dislike Rowan. Jack was trying to be far more controlling than Rowan ever was.

  Quietly I sat down in my seat in physiology class beside Kayla. Although Jack was in the class, we had assigned seating, so we couldn't sit next to each other. Not that I would have wanted to sit with him at the moment anyway. Gently I opened my textbook and pulled my notebook out of my backpack. We had a substitute teacher who didn't look like she knew where she was or what she was supposed to be doing. She appeared to be trying to figure out what class she was currently in. Being familiar with these situations, I doubted we would be starting anytime soon. Sighing, I resisted the urge to roll my eyes.

  "Hey, what's up with you?" Kayla asked. "I saw that you and Jack didn't walk in together."

"Oh, it's nothing." I looked back down into my book, trying to show that I wasn't interested in talking. It didn't seem to be working.

"Does it have anything to do with Rowan?" She was obviously fishing for gossip.

I really didn't want to have this conversation, but from the look on her face, I didn't have much of a choice. I closed my book and put it on my desk. There would be rumors whether I talked about it or not, so I might as well try to make the rumors more true than not.

"Okay, yeah. Ever since I started going out with Rowan, Jack hasn't been himself. Usually, he's fun and sweet, but now he's ultra controlling. He acts like I can't talk or spend time with anyone who isn't him. And on top of that, he seems to have something against Rowan. Something very specific to him. He says he heard rumors that Rowan cheated on his ex last year, and that's why he doesn't think I should be with him, but I feel like that's just an excuse." I realized that I had been rambling, but it kinda felt good to get it out.

"His ex. He dated that Delilah girl last year, right? She's literally hotter than any model I've ever seen. I can't imagine why he'd cheat on her," Kayla said.

"You're telling me," I mumbled.

"Well, I can tell you what the problem is." She looked down at her pointy acrylic nails, examining them.

I looked at her, puzzled.

"Isn't it obvious? Jack's jealous," she said.

I laughed, rolling my eyes. "No way. We're just friends, best friends. Neither of us have feelings like that."

"Hear me out," she said. "He's been following you around for the past four years like some kind of a lost puppy.

You've dated a couple guys on and off, but Jack's never been with anyone. I mean, it's kind of depressing. He's been waiting for you to fall in love with him for four years. Now that you're finally in a serious relationship, he's jealous. I'm not saying that he's right for trying to keep you from being with Rowan, but it is understandable."

As much as I didn't want to believe it, what she was saying actually made a lot of sense. I felt kinda stupid for not thinking about it before.

"I guess I never put all of those pieces together before. I was so used to the idea of him being my best friend, my brother, that I couldn't imagine he could feel anything more for me." I was surprised that I'd been so oblivious. I'd always thought of myself as someone who noticed small things like that.

She looked at me with sympathy, the way one might look at a disappointed kindergartener. "Don't look now, but he's staring at you."

I turned around and met Jack's eyes. There was something more than friendship in them. The emotion was so raw, so clear, that it almost hurt to look into them. He looked at me with what seemed to be adoration. After a few seconds, he looked away. I could see disappointment, and also fear, in his eyes. He looked angry, not at me, but with himself. It hurt me to see him distressed in that way, especially since I was the one causing the pain. I turned back around, not sure what to think about what I'd just seen.

"He always looks at you like that. Like you're the greatest thing on Earth." Kayla smiled. It was a sad smile, like she was watching the world burn but couldn't help but recognize the beauty in the flames. "I thought you knew," she said quietly.

"I had no idea." I ran my hand through my hair, pulling on it in frustration.

"There are worse things, you know. I can imagine so many things that would be worse than having two gorgeous guys desperately in love with me," Kayla sighed.

I thought about what she'd said. I'd never really paid attention to the way Jack looked before. He was objectively very handsome. His beauty was almost the exact opposite of Rowan's. Where Rowan was tan with golden hair, Jack was pale with hair blacker than a raven. Rowan was muscular and heavily built. Jack was slender with a figure so frail that it could have been a girl's. There was beauty in both—I could acknowledge that and accept it. But my heart saw no one other than Rowan. I loved him wholly and completely. There was simply no room left for anyone else. Jack was my best friend, but that was all he would ever be. I couldn't change that even if I wanted to. Some people simply weren't meant to be more than friends.

Kayla interrupted my thoughts and brought me back to the present. "So what are you going to do? I can tell from the look on your face that you don't love Jack."

Not knowing what else to do, I sighed. "No, not in that way. It's different, I love him as a best friend, nothing more. Still, I just hate the thought of hurting him. He's been a constant presence in my life for years. Honestly, I never really had a best friend before him, and I couldn't imagine replacing him. But I don't think he'd want to stick around, always coming second in my heart. It wouldn't be fair to him. I don't know what I'm going to do, but I do know that I love Rowan. I love him more than I can put into words. He's meant for me in a way that Jack isn't."

"I hate to say it," Kayla said, "but you're probably going to have to pick. It's not in a man's nature to sit around being second in line when he could be first for someone else."

"Yeah, I'm starting to realize that," I said.

I sat in my backyard, plucking up strands of grass and tearing them to shreds. How could I have been so hopelessly clueless for four years? How had I not noticed that the guy I'd spent every single day with was in love with me? It all made perfect sense now. Jack never having a girlfriend, choosing all of the same electives as me, going to prom with me last year, as friends. And this year, was his prom invitation an attempt to tell me how he felt? In exasperation, I threw myself back against the grass and rubbed my face. Suddenly I had a strong urge to bang my head against the nearest tree. In the past month, I'd discovered that my boyfriend was a faerie, that he had a drop-dead gorgeous ex-girlfriend who wanted him back, and that my best friend was in love with me. In truth, I wouldn't have minded so much except that I was going to have to hurt Jack. And I was *fairly* sure killing your boyfriend's ex was still classified as murder.

Angrily I picked up a pinecone and threw it across the yard. No matter what I did, someone was going to get hurt. Now I realized I'd taken Jack's friendship for granted all of these years. For years I'd expected that he'd always be there when I needed him, whether it was to talk about books or make me feel better after I'd had my heart broken. But now I realized that the whole time I'd been with Rowan, I'd been breaking Jack's heart. I'd thought he was being controlling and selfish, when really he'd just been jealous. In an amusing turn of events, I had prided myself on being an observant person when it came to figuring out that Rowan was a faerie, but I'd been oblivious to the fact that Jack had been in love with me for years.

It was impossible to ignore the irony. Lily Rhodes, the smartest girl in school, hadn't had her nose out of a book long enough to notice that her best friend had been in love with her for four years. In a strange way, I almost wished that I'd never found out because now that I knew, I was going to have to break his heart. But I also knew that breaking his heart would break mine. Honestly, I probably deserved it. There was a chance I might lose Jack forever. He might decide that I wasn't worth his time after he knew there wasn't any hope for us in the way he wanted there to be. The one thing I knew was that I was going to have to tell him. It would be painful to have to tell him I knew how he felt, but it didn't change anything. It was certain that I was still going to be with Rowan. Suddenly I remembered Jack's eyes in class earlier that day. They were the same eyes that had been my biggest comfort for years, but they were filled with pain because of me. It was a little sick, but I just hoped I had the courage to break his heart.

Chapter 13
FRIENDS

Saturday came, and it was time for my shopping trip with Ginger and Giselle. Truthfully I was still feeling kind of depressed, as well as guilty about Jack, and I wasn't in much of a mood for shopping. After a bit of consideration, I had decided not to mention anything about Jack being in love with me to Rowan. Knowing Rowan, I didn't think he would mind, but he would probably want me to confront Jack about it. Jack continued to call every day, but every time I just sat holding my phone in my hands, waiting for it to stop ringing. It might have been silly, but I was afraid the emotion in my voice would reveal that I knew about his feelings for me. There was a large part of me that just wasn't ready for that conversation yet. In some ways, I wished that I could forget I'd ever found out. Unfortunately, no matter how hard I tried, the memory of that conversation with Kayla was always at the front of my mind. It was like watching a horrific event occur before your eyes and not being able to unsee it later. Every time I closed my eyes, I saw Jack's desperate expression from that day in physiology class.

Rowan was the only thing that had been able to distract me. I could forget about Jack when I was with Rowan. He helped me remember that although I missed Jack the way you might miss a lost limb, my heart was still intact with Rowan by my side. I knew I wouldn't feel whole again until I could have both of them at the same time.

I looked out my bedroom window and saw that Ginger and Giselle had just arrived. I looked in the mirror, trying to make sure that my fake smile was convincing enough.

I led Ginger and Giselle up to my room, where they proceeded to examine everything I owned as if it were the most interesting thing they'd ever seen.

"I've never been in a human's house before!" Giselle picked up one of my necklaces, carefully scrutinizing it. "Not nearly sparkly enough."

Ginger turned to look at me and gasped. "What has happened to your hair!"

I immediately reached up to touch the ponytail on top of my head. As far as I knew, there was nothing wrong with my hair. I'd looked in the mirror not five minutes before, and it had been perfectly normal.

"Oh my!" Giselle put her hand over her mouth.

"What?!" I shouted.

"You weren't going to leave the house with it like that, were you?" Ginger asked.

"Well, actually I was —"

They both ran over to me and pushed me down onto my bed. Before I knew it, my hair was down around my face, and Giselle was grabbing a curling iron out of a large, pink, sparkly bag she had brought with her. Ginger was arranging a whole pile of makeup pallets that she had taken out of the same bag.

"Don't worry, we're going to fix you." Giselle began slowly wrapping my hair around the curling iron.

"Do you always carry that much, uh, stuff with you?" I looked at the selection of things that she had taken out of the bag. I doubted that I'd ever owned that much makeup in my life, much less all at one time.

"Oh, yes, we always carry around a small amount of supplies in case of emergencies. We brought a little extra because we thought you might need a few touch ups. But we didn't think you'd be this desperate!" Ginger said, sounding exasperated.

She began to apply a layer of primer to my face, quickly moving onto foundation and highlighter. I wasn't sure if I should be insulted by their apparent lack of confidence in my ability to take care of my appearance or not. I felt like a Barbie doll whose owner happened to be the well trained daughter of a makeup artist. I'd never paid much attention to what Ginger and Giselle wore before now. But seeing as I was temporarily their captive, I didn't have much else to do. Giselle was impeccably dressed in a floor length purple dress that was covered in a variety of different colored flowers. Her hair was in its naturally curly state, but small portions of it had been pulled back to create several different braids that joined together in the back. Her shoes were black sandals that laced up to her mid-calf. In stark contrast, Ginger wore black jeans along with a dark green peasant-style blouse. She had on high heeled black boots that went up past her knees. Unlike Giselle, she hadn't let her hair stay in its natural curls. Ginger's hair was straightened and clipped back on the sides with butterfly-shaped golden pins. Both of them had on an array of jewelry, each personalized to match their outfit. There was no doubt that they were stunning. But if I was expected to dress like that every day, I would probably collapse on the floor surrounded by sparkly clothes after the first week.

"All right, we're done. The only thing you have to do

now is change clothes," Ginger announced.

"Change clothes?" I asked.

"Mhm, although I'm discovering that your closet is desperately lacking," Giselle said from somewhere within the depths of my closet.

I sighed, resigning myself to their plans. I walked over to my mirror, examining myself. They had actually done a really good job. My hair flowed freely around me in gentle but defined curls. My makeup looked professionally done, but it made me slightly uncomfortable since I'd never worn this much before. My eyeshadow was a mix of pink and gold, with a thin line of eyeliner and a generous amount of mascara. My cheeks were heavily contoured with far more blush than I would have chosen to apply. Still, I couldn't say it looked bad. The necklace Rowan had given me was hanging around my neck, and it seemed to highlight my entire appearance. Giselle threw me a wad of clothes and ordered me into the bathroom to change.

I finished changing and looked down at myself. She had given me a navy blue shirt-dress that tied with a cloth belt around the waist. She'd also given me black tights and a pair of black boots I was fairly sure I'd never seen before. I was highly suspicious that the boots had come out of the sparkly pink bag without my notice. Despite everything, I thought I looked good. Probably a lot better than I would have made myself look if I hadn't had their help.

The first store we went into was a complete disaster. Everything in the place was either so short that you couldn't sit down in it or so low in the front that I couldn't physically manage to get it to stay up. The second store was far more successful. Ginger and Giselle practically ran through the aisles, grabbing handfuls of clothes off the shelves. I didn't even get the chance to take a single dress off the rack before they shoved me into the dressing room. They had given me a pile of dresses that was practically tall enough to be a mountain. I looked under the dressing room door to see Giselle jumping up and down, animatedly talking about some sort of new lipstick. I looked down at the pile of clothes in front of me and decided it was time to get to work.

The first three dresses I tried on were all too pink and sparkly. I carefully set them aside without mentioning them to either Ginger or Giselle. The next dress was a golden ball gown style dress. Surprisingly, I liked the design, but I was afraid the color would make me look even more pale. Next was a pale blue, empire-waist dress with lace accents. Although I usually loved dresses of this style, I found myself bored with the idea of wearing this one. I wanted something that would impress Rowan, and this was just not it.

The last dress I tried on was a blood-red, mermaid-style dress. It was covered in sequins, so I was sure it would meet with both Ginger and Giselle's approval. It was also sleeveless, which I normally wouldn't have liked, but this dress was different. I felt beautiful in this dress. Beautiful enough to outshine even Delilah. The dress seemed a perfect fit to every part of my body but didn't make me look lumpy as most tight dresses did. I modeled the dress for each of the girls, who squealed with approval. They both commented on how gorgeous the dress made me look and swarmed around me like bees, making sure it had no rips or tears. We left the store, all happily content, and loaded the dress into their car.

Ginger sat in the driver's seat while Giselle sat in the back with me. She seemed like she might never stop talking.

"Oh Lily, that dress is so pretty, and it makes you look wonderful. I'm sure that Rowan will be very impressed. Now, of course, you'll have to let us come over early before prom so that we can get you ready. Do you want your hair curled, or should we put it up?"

I was looking out the window, completely lost in thought. It had been a good distraction to go shopping, but I had forgotten about the dress, and my mind had gone back to Jack.

"Lily, what's wrong? Are you okay?" Giselle asked.

"Yeah, I'm fine. I was just out of it for a second. Oh, and I think I probably want my hair —"

"Lily, forget about the hair." Giselle put her hand on my arm. "I can tell something's wrong. You can tell us." She looked at Ginger, who smiled and nodded.

Other than Jack and Rowan, these two were the closest thing to friends I'd ever had. If I could talk about my situation with Kayla, I could talk about it with them.

"It's my best friend, Jack. He's in love with me, but I don't want to hurt him by telling him I don't feel the same way. I don't know how I could live without him, but he refuses to tolerate Rowan. I'm stuck between the two. I just don't want to hurt anyone, but I know I have to, and that it's going to be Jack who gets hurt." I let out a breath. It did feel good to talk about it.

"Well, I can't tell you there's a way to fix your problem. But maybe I can explain Jack's frustration towards Rowan in a way that will make more sense. Jack feels the same way about Rowan as Delilah feels about you. Despite how much of a despicable person she is, she does have feelings. She's jealous of you because you get to be with the person she loves. She hates you for it because you have the one thing she wants. Jack probably feels the same way about Rowan," Giselle said.

"There's literally no way that Delilah is jealous of me."

"But there is," Ginger interjected. "Not in the typical way that women are jealous of each other, but in a different way. A much more painful way. She doesn't envy you for your beauty or your clothes or anything like that. She's jealous of you because you have the one she loves. You were successful in making Rowan love you, which was something she could never do."

"He was never happy with her, always lonely looking," Giselle added.

"That sounds like a terrible sort of pain, a pain I hate putting Jack through." I ran my hand through my hair, tugging at it in frustration.

"But that's just it, Lily. You're not putting him through that pain. He's putting himself through it. It's not your fault he fell in love with you. If he truly loves you as you think he does, then he'll learn to accept that you're happy with someone else. He'll grow to be content with the idea that you are as happy as you could possibly be. In time, that will make him happy too." Giselle took my hand, squeezing it.

We smiled at each other. I had underestimated both of them. On the surface, they appeared childish; when it came to things that mattered, they were better than a therapist. They weren't just close to my friends, they were my friends.

What Ginger and Giselle had said made me feel less guilty about Jack. I knew it wasn't my fault that he was in this situation. I felt more sorry for him now than I did guilty. But I still missed him with the same ferocity that I had before. In an odd way, I felt pity for Delilah as well. I knew she wasn't a nice person; Ginger and Giselle had affirmed my opinions on that. I just couldn't help but feel sorry for any person who was living in true misery and disappointment, even if it was Delilah.

Chapter 14
Mascara and Tears

After my talk with Ginger and Giselle, I went home and called Jack, but he didn't answer. All week I tried calling him several times a day, but he never picked up the phone. When I tried to talk to him at school, he avoided eye contact and walked away. We hadn't said one word to each other since our fight, and I didn't know how to fix it. We'd never gone more than a couple days without talking. Before Rowan became a part of my life, Jack and I were inseparable. Now it was as if he was trying to convince himself that I had never existed. I knew I'd been wrong not to accept his apologies right after we fought, but I couldn't go back and change that. I just missed my best friend. I didn't care anymore if he never wanted to talk to Rowan. I'd gladly go my whole life keeping the two of them separate if I could just have both of them.

I woke up on Saturday, the day of prom, to see Ginger and Giselle standing over me. I sat up in bed, rubbed my eyes, and looked over at the alarm clock. It was only six thirty! They'd woken me up at six thirty, on a Saturday!

"Why did you get me up so early?" I groaned.

My hair was surrounding my face in a large ball of tangles, and there were dark circles under my eyes.

"It's prom!" Giselle squealed.

"We need to have time to get you ready." Ginger pulled a large hairbrush out of one of the many bags they had dropped on the floor. She started brushing my hair, yanking all the tangles out. My bangs were standing up in all sorts of crazy ways, and I attempted to pat them down.

"Wait, how did you get in my house?" I asked.

"Oh, your mom let us in. She's such a nice lady. She helped us plan the whole day!" Giselle said, excitedly.

"She did?" I asked.

My mom wasn't much of a planner. She was usually lucky to remember what day of the week it was.

"Mhm, your hair, makeup, and nails are all supposed to be done by ten. At ten, we'll have brunch with your parents. After brunch, we'll put your dress on. Rowan should be here around eleven thirty for pictures. Pictures will probably take several hours, so we'll take a break in the middle for snacks. After we're finished with pictures, you and Rowan are going out to dinner, and then prom." Ginger finished brushing my hair and pulled me up off the bed.

"So, uh, do I actually have to do anything today?" I asked.

"Yes, three things. Look pretty, don't mess up our work, and take a shower." Giselle pushed me into the bathroom, giving me directions to wash my hair.

At least I didn't have to do anything. I just had to be Barbie again for the day.

I got out of the shower, my hair falling like a wet towel around me. I dried myself off and put on a pair of leggings and a sweater. I went back into my room and was immediately ambushed by Ginger holding a hairdryer and Giselle holding a strange looking hairbrush. They pulled me onto my bed and started drying my hair. As soon as my hair was dry, Giselle began curling it, the same way she had when we went shopping. Ginger started on my makeup, having to stop me from falling asleep several times. I heard them talking to each other, mostly about the popular gossip of the week.

My thoughts drifted off, ignoring what was happening around me. Truthfully I didn't care much what they did. What I really wanted was to be alone with Rowan. Every part of me desperately missed Jack, and although I liked spending time with Ginger and Giselle, Rowan was the only one who could make me stop thinking about him. Rowan was like a protective shield. When I was around him, all of my problems seemed to fade away, and the only thing that was left was our love.

What seemed like an eternity later, Ginger told me they were finished. I looked at myself in the mirror. It really did look beautiful. My hair flowed down to my waist in a curtain of shiny curls. My makeup was obviously designed to look both natural and done-up. Considering my general lack of female know-how, I wasn't really sure how you accomplished both at the same time, but it looked good. They'd even done my nails without my noticing. My nails were short, the way I liked to keep them. Throughout my whole life, I had been repulsed by the idea of pointy nails. They were painted a bright red with crimson sparkles. Generally, I didn't like high-maintenance looking nails, but I did like these.

Smiling at myself in the mirror, I noticed that what made me look the most beautiful was a smile that reached all the way up into my eyes. But I knew I couldn't manage a smile like that at the moment; I was missing Jack too much. When I was with Rowan, I was sure I would look more beautiful than I ever had before.

We went downstairs for brunch. Ginger and Giselle

both greeted my mom as though they had been friends for life. Like me, my mom was very antisocial. She normally spent her time at the bookstore, either reading or working — usually both at the same time. But with Ginger and Giselle, she looked like the most outgoing person in the world. They really could talk a brick wall into wearing a ball gown. We sat in the dining room, Ginger and Giselle on either side of me and my parents across from us. My dad, as usual, was ignoring the rest of us, reading a magazine about the best new book releases of the year, which blocked his face from everyone else. I sipped my coffee, not feeling very hungry.

"Oh, Lily honey, you look so pretty. You girls did a wonderful job on her hair. There's so much to work with that even when she was little, I could never get it to curl. Now, which one of you is which again?"

Over the course of the meal, my mom probably asked them what their names were ten different times. We sat around eating for another half hour. Ginger and Giselle did most of the talking, while my mom kept trying to remember their names. I mostly listened. I did learn some interesting information, though. Ginger had been engaged to a guy for a year, probably a faerie, who lived in New York City. They were planning to get married next summer. He was going to move here, and they were going to rent an apartment in town. Both Ginger and Giselle worked as party planners, which didn't surprise me even a little. Listening to them talk, I realized that I hadn't asked them many questions about themselves. I made a mental note to ask them about it the next time we saw each other.

We finished eating, and they rushed me back upstairs to put my dress on. I only wore one piece of jewelry, the necklace that Rowan had given me. Giselle tried to convince me to wear a pair of long sparkly earnings, but I told her she would have to hold me down to get those things on me. For a second, I thought she was seriously considering it. Thankfully, she got distracted with curling a piece of my hair that she had missed earlier. I had just finished putting my dress on, which still looked as mesmerizing as it had the first time I'd worn it, when I realized I didn't have any shoes.

"I'll just wear a pair of flats," I said.

"Oh no you won't." Giselle stood between me and my closet, looking like she might tackle me if I reached for the flats.

"We brought a whole selection for you to choose from." Ginger pulled open a bag full of silver sparkly shoes.

"You guys know I can't walk in heels. I'll trip and fall in front of everyone." I looked into the bag, which seemed to contain only shoes with at least a five-inch heel.

Ginger stuck her hand into the bag, which looked a bit like a bottomless pit, evidently searching for something specific. "I found them!" She pulled out a pair of silver wedge heels. They had one strap around the top and one around the ankle. The heel looked to be about two inches. I looked at both of the girls skeptically.

"Please, Lily, try them for us!" Giselle batted her eyelashes. Ginger smiled hopefully at me.

I sighed. "All right."

I sat on my bed, careful not to mess up my dress, and slid the shoes onto my feet. I fastened the straps and stood up. It felt better than I had expected, but I was still nervous. They both smiled at me, practically beaming. I felt a bit like a piece of art being admired by its creators.

We heard a car pull into the driveway, and Giselle rushed over toward the window. "It's Rowan, he's early!" Giselle looked as if she might get sick.

Ginger hurriedly adjusted my hair and the ruffles on the bottom of my dress. As soon as she was done, they grabbed my hands and pulled me down the stairs. I realized I knew exactly what it was like to have not one faerie godmother, but two.

Rowan was already inside talking to my mom when we got downstairs. His eyes met mine on the steps, and for the first time all day, I felt like I really smiled. His eyes moved away from mine, looking at the rest of me. I suddenly felt very self-conscious, remembering how Delilah had looked in that black dress. He looked back up at me, smiling, but differently now. It wasn't a happy smile, but rather an adoring one. Maybe I didn't have any reason to be self-conscious. I smiled back and walked over to hug him.

"Absolutely no hugging before pictures," Giselle said, holding a camera she had seemingly produced out of thin air.

"I guess we have our orders," Rowan grinned, offering me his arm to walk outside. We walked out to the back yard, and as I had earlier predicted, I tripped. I stepped on the bottom part of my dress and started falling forward. Rowan reached out and caught me before I hit the ground.

"Heels, huh?" He grinned, setting me back on the ground.

"Not my choice," I mumbled, shooting an evil glare back at both of the girls.

Rowan laughed. Neither of them seemed to notice as they were looking down at both a boutonnière and the corsage that Ginger was holding. I was convinced that they could literally conjure things up when they needed them. They had definitely not walked out of the house with either of those.

Rowan untucked my hair from behind my ear and whispered to me, "You look beautiful. I have to admit I didn't expect you to look quite that good in your dress, but you blew away all of my expectations."

I smiled up at him. I hadn't paid much attention to what he was wearing before, but now I was. He was dressed in a plain black tux with a black shirt and a red bow tie.

"You dress to impress," I said.

"Always," he whispered in my ear.

"All right, you two, listen up." Giselle looked more serious than I'd ever seen her before. I was tempted to laugh. "I want you to stand over in front of that tree and put these on each other."

Ginger handed me the boutonnière and Rowan the corsage.

"Yes, ma'am," Rowan whispered under his breath.

I laughed, and he grinned down at me. We walked over to the tree, and Rowan started to put the corsage around my wrist. It was a simple design, red roses and baby's breath. But they seemed perfect for us. I wouldn't have wanted something extravagant. He finished attaching it to my wrist and kissed my cheek. I blushed, but I wasn't sure if anyone could tell with all the makeup I had on. I heard the steady clicking of a camera and smiled up at him. The least I could do was make the pictures look good. I started to attach the boutonnière, but my hands were shaking too much.

"Need help?" Rowan asked.

"Please," I said.

He put his hands over mine, steadying them. My hands

stopped shaking, and I was able to clip it onto his jacket.

He tilted my head up toward him with his hand. "I love you."

"I love you, too," I said.

For the next several hours, we were at the mercy of Giselle, who kept herding us around like cattle. Ginger shot us several sympathetic looks, but they didn't do us much good until she brought us cookies, which gave us an excuse to take a break. Having not eaten much at breakfast, I ate lots of cookies. I wasn't very concerned whether the crumbs got on the dress or not. We already had tons of pictures. Eventually, I got so many crumbs on me that Giselle laid an array of napkins on my lap, grumbling about messing up her work. Rowan thought this was hysterical.

We finished eating and were sent back out into the yard to take more pictures. About an hour later, Rowan said that we were going to miss our dinner reservation if we didn't leave. I was pretty sure it was just an excuse to get out of more picture taking, but I didn't care. Ginger, Giselle, and my mom all hugged me, telling me to have a good time. We left happily, which surprised me in some small way. A few months ago, if someone had told me that I would be going to prom with the love of my life, I would have laughed at them.

Rowan selected a Mexican restaurant, which I was thrilled about. There were dozens of other couples dressed for prom scattered around us, but all I could see was Rowan. Both of us ate like we'd never seen food before, concluding that taking pictures must make you hungry. Several of the other girls sitting near us gawked at how much we were eating. He and I just laughed at them, saying that if you couldn't even eat in front of your date, you probably shouldn't have gone with them at all. Both of us finished eating in a rush, ready to get away from all of the awkward looking couples who couldn't even manage to make eye contact with each other. We practically ran back out to his car hand-in-hand, laughing.

Rowan and I went into prom, which was being held in the school gym. A lot of the girls had complained that it wasn't somewhere else, but I didn't care where it was, as long as Rowan was there with me. Both of us sat for a while talking and laughing. As soon as the first slow song came on, we were out of our seats faster than lightning. He held my hand as we went into the center of the room, looking only at each other. Neither of us cared when the song ended, and a faster pace song came on. We kept slow dancing. He held me against him, only letting go to spin me around or kiss me. I felt like I was in another world. A world full of princes, princesses, knights, and faeries. I wasn't sure if Rowan was a prince or a faerie in that world. I didn't take my attention off him long enough to think about it.

After a long time, we went to sit down. Rowan went to get us something to drink while I took a moment to rest. I looked around the room. The music was so loud you could barely hear the person next to you talking. Groups of people, mostly girls, were dancing. Most of the couples had sat down to eat or drink. There were small huddles of people standing against the wall. One particular group of boys was very noisy. They were laughing, and a few of them were shoving each other. I rolled my eyes. It was probably a group of football players who couldn't manage to find dates.

I was about to look away when a pair of silver eyes caught my attention. Jack was standing in the center of the group, his carefree smile changed into a shocked expression.

It was like I was on auto-pilot. I stood up, not breaking eye contact with him, and started walking in his direction. His shock turned to panic, and he seemed to start looking for a way to get away without my noticing. I walked up to him, looking up into his eyes. He looked at me, beads of sweat running down his face. Suddenly the room wasn't so loud or so dark. It seemed as though we were the only two people in the room.

He opened his mouth. "Lily...."

"Is this the girl we've heard so much about?" the boy standing to the right of Jack asked.

His eyes looked me up and down, staring in a way that I didn't like. A few of the other boys in the group laughed. They were all holding drinks in their hands that sloshed on the floor as they shook with laughter. Jack moved to stand between me and the boy on his right.

"Lily, you need to go away." Jack took my arm, leading me away from the group.

"No." I shook my arm free of his hand.

"Lily, I'm serious." Jack moved to grab my arm again, but one of the other boys did first. He pulled me closer to him, smiling sickly. There was sweat running down his face, his hair was sticking up in all directions, and I could smell alcohol on his breath. Anger swelled up inside me. I yanked my arm free and kicked him as hard as I could. He bent over in pain, spilling his drink all over my dress. The other boys' faces seemed to vary between surprise and fear.

I looked at Jack. "Are you coming with me, or are you staying with these drunken idiots?"

The boy I had kicked was still rubbing his leg, keeping his eyes on the ground. If I hadn't been so angry, I might have been proud of myself.

Jack looked down, not meeting my eyes. "Lily, I...I...."

I felt the tears begin to fall down my cheeks. "Don't bother. You're only supposed to be my best friend anyway."

He started to look up at me, but I turned around and walked away. As soon as I was away from them, I let the tears fall. I touched my face. My fingers were black from the mascara mixed with tears.

I felt a hand touch my arm. I raised my fist, ready to punch.

"Whoa, whoa, it's just me!" Athena was standing in front of me with both hands raised.

I lowered my fist, embarrassed.

"I saw you walk away from those guys crying. I wanted to make sure you were okay. Their drinks are spiked. I saw the boy who snuck it in." She lowered her hands and saw the place where he'd spilled his drink on my dress. "Lily, are you okay? Do I need to get someone?" I could see the fear in her eyes.

"No, I'm okay, really...." The room started to spin, and I began to fall backward.

Then two arms went around me, and I heard Athena tell Rowan what had happened. He said something back to her, but I couldn't tell what it was. I was too dizzy. I heard Rowan murmuring things to me; he kept saying my name.

"Lily, just stay with me. I've got you, Lily. Lily, I need you to stay awake until I can get you to the car. Lily, can you hear me? Say something if you can hear me. Lily...." He kept talking, but I could only hear parts of what he said. My vision went in and out of focus. I was faintly aware that Athena was following us, keeping people at a distance. We went out the door and started toward the parking lot. I thought I heard Jack yell my name. I tried to turn around to look, but I couldn't stand up any longer. I began falling toward the ground, and I felt Rowan's arms wrap around me. He picked me up, carrying me the way he had on the day I had met him. Then everything went black.

I came back to consciousness in my room. I heard Rowan saying he had called Ginger and Giselle and that they were on their way. My mom was crying, and my dad was mumbling something under his breath. I opened my eyes and saw them all huddled by my bedroom door. I was still in my dress, but the makeup had been cleaned off my face. They all seemed to notice that I was awake and stopped talking. I tried to sit up but fell back onto my bed. I heard my mom gasp as Rowan rushed toward me. He sat on my bed beside me, gently running his hand through my hair.

"How are you?" he asked.

"Dizzy, tired, confused." I reached up to take his hand in mine.

He half-smiled, gently holding my hand. "I know you really wanted to go to the picnic tomorrow with my family, but I think you should stay here and rest. You went into shock earlier. I've called Ginger and Giselle. They're on their way so they can spend the night with you." He smiled gently, but it was a worried smile.

With all that had happened, I'd completely forgotten about the picnic. He'd told me about it a week ago, but it had just slipped my mind. Even though I doubted that I'd be completely better in the morning, I still wanted to go. The idea of being around Marie and the rest of Rowan's family comforted me.

"No, I want to go. Ginger and Giselle can drive me, and we'll meet you there." I looked at him, attempting a smile.

"If that's what you really want." He sounded nervous about the idea, but I knew he wouldn't fight with me about it.

"It is," I said.

I saw Ginger and Giselle walk into the room. They stood beside my parents near my bedroom door.

"I'll see you tomorrow. I love you, Lily." He leaned forward and kissed my forehead.

"I love you too," I said.

He smiled at me and left. A moment later, Ginger, Giselle, and my mom were huddled around my bed. My dad continued to stand awkwardly by the door staring at his shoes, until my mom told him to leave so that I could change.

Giselle helped me out of my dress and gave me a pair of sweatpants and a T-shirt to put on. At that moment, I couldn't have imagined a better pair of clothes. Ginger brushed my hair, which was tangled and covered in sweat. My mom brought us three cups of tea from the kitchen and a wet washcloth to wipe off my face. They sat with me, talking about books, food, school, anything to distract me. My mom continued to carry endless cups of tea up to my room for as long as we stayed awake. We talked for about two hours until I managed to fall asleep.

I woke up many times during the night, sometimes calling for Rowan and at other times calling for Jack. I could never remember what my nightmares were about, just that I'd needed one of them to save me. Each time I woke up either crying, screaming, or sometimes both. But every single time, Ginger and Giselle were both there. They sat on the sides of my bed, holding my hands. Ginger, who had a very pretty voice, would sing lullabies to get me back to sleep. Giselle, who wasn't very good at singing, would simply hum along. They were the most amazing friends I could have asked for.

Chapter 15
LIFE WITHOUT YOU

I woke up the next morning and looked around the room. Ginger was slumped over in my comfy chair in the corner of the room. She was still wearing her clothes from the previous day and looked as if she hadn't been asleep very long. Giselle was lying on the floor beside my bed with a pillow over her head. She was also still in the same clothes she had worn the night before, but she had taken her heels off and traded them for a pair of fuzzy socks. They both looked exhausted. I felt bad for keeping them up all night, but I didn't think I could have made it without them. I thought we'd been close before, but I now knew that they were probably the most devoted friends I'd ever had. Especially now that Jack had seemingly ended our friendship.

Jack.... Thinking about him was like shoving a dagger into my heart. He'd been my everything for four years. He'd saved my life. Before Jack, I hadn't had any friends. I'd been totally alone. Sure, there had been people that I'd talked to at school, but no one that I could truly bare my soul to. Jack had been like my twin flame. Losing him was like losing a piece of myself. He'd been there for me through everything, except for this. The worst part was, he hadn't only turned away from me, he'd traded my friendship for the type of people we'd always fought against. The boys he'd been with last night, they were the type of people we'd promised ourselves we'd never be. In tenth grade, Jack had organized a Drug Free Clubs of America event, and now he was hanging out with people that smuggled alcohol onto school property. It's not like he was discouraging their behavior either; he'd been participating in it. He wasn't acting like the Jack I knew, the Jack that had been my best friend. He had never done anything like this before.

A horrible thought suddenly occurred to me. What if I'd driven him to this? What if his jealousy, loneliness, and despair at my not loving him back had caused him to go down this path? What if he was throwing his life away because of me. His eyes had looked grief-stricken last night, as if he'd lost someone. That, someone, had to be me. Not that he'd lost me in the literal sense, but he'd lost the possibility of my loving him. Maybe he'd finally accepted what I'd been asking him to all this time, that I was in love with Rowan. And with that, he'd realized that I'd never love him, not in the way he wanted me to. But I hadn't denied him friendship; he'd denied that for himself. I had gone after him, urging him to come with me. I had to know that he had been the one to turn me away. That was his choice. Even though it was a result of his feelings for me, I was not the one at fault. He'd accepted my choice to be with Rowan. Now I had to accept his.

My feet softly hit the floor as I made my way to the bathroom, careful not to wake anyone up. First, I took a shower, washing all of the sweat from the previous night off my body and out of my hair. Somehow I wished that I could wash away the memories, too. Quietly I dried my hair, something I rarely took the time to do. After drying it, I braided it into three dutch-braids from the crown of my head to the nape of my neck. I tied the braids off, pinning the rest of my hair into a tight bun.

There was no way I would allow myself to act like a victim. Yes, I had lost Jack, and getting over him would take more time than I could probably imagine. But I couldn't forget what I still had and what I had gained. Rowan, the new constant rock in my life, was still with me. He was what I'd always dreamed of finding but never thought I actually would find. The way he'd taken care of me last night proved that he was chivalrous and responsible, qualities that few modern men had. There was no doubt that I was lucky to have him as my own. And I'd gained two of the most loving friends in the world, Ginger and Giselle. It was incredible to think that I could hardly imagine my life without them now. Although my life had become more complicated with the addition of faeries, it had also been made far more exciting. Like most nerdy girls, I'd always inwardly wished for an adventure like the ones in books. This must have been my adventure. But I'd never fully understood how difficult adventures were for the characters experiencing them. Not until I was experiencing my own. It was far more complicated to live the adventure when it was occurring in your own world. It was terrifying that I couldn't simply close a book and go back to how my life had been before. As impossible as it seemed, I had to be my own heroine now.

With a steady hand, I applied a generous amount of eyeliner and mascara, something I wouldn't have normally done. But today, I wanted to feel powerful.

Clearing my mind, I went to my closet and took out a black, knee-length sundress and my black sandals. I put them on and went downstairs. I took a steady breath before looking at the time. It was a few minutes after eleven. After opening the fridge, I took out some eggs and started frying them. We weren't supposed to meet Rowan's family for several more hours, and I was too hungry to wait that long to eat.

A while later, Ginger and Giselle came into the kitchen together. They had both changed clothes and redone their hair and makeup. My eyes met theirs while I was leaning on the counter, eating a plate of eggs.

"You look way better," Giselle yawned.

"Are you sure you're well enough to go?" Ginger asked. "It's just a picnic. No one would blame you if you wanted to rest instead." She poured two glasses of orange juice and handed one to Giselle.

"No, I'm really feeling much better. It'll be nice to be around everyone again." I finished my eggs, putting my plate in the sink.

My mom walked into the kitchen with a surprised expression on her face. She hadn't changed out of her sweatpants, and her hair was clearly unbrushed.

"I didn't expect you three to be awake yet, considering how late you were up last night. Are you sure you want to go today?" she asked.

"I'm sure." I smiled, trying to show them that I didn't want to be treated differently than any other day.

Yesterday was the ending, the time for crying. Today was simply the start of something new.

Chapter 16
THE PICNIC

Ginger, Giselle, and I left my house and drove to Rowan's. We pulled into his driveway and saw that everyone else had already arrived. I worried for a moment that we might have been extremely late, then I remembered that everyone else only had to walk a few houses down the street to get there. Rowan opened the car door for me, smiling. As soon as I stepped out, he pulled me into a tight hug. It wasn't the type of hug you would normally give someone you saw every day. It was the type of hug that you gave someone who you hadn't seen for months or years.

"I'm sorry I left last night," he whispered into my ear. "I just thought you might rather be around girls. How are you feeling?" He looked at me quizzically, as if he thought I might have some sort of underlying disease.

I sighed. Would no one ever believe that I was capable of keeping my emotions under control?

"I'm fine, really. I feel great." I smiled at him and leaned forward to give him a kiss on the cheek.

He tilted my head away from his cheek and toward his lips. He wrapped his arms around me and kissed me. After a few seconds, I pulled away and started laughing. After watching me laugh, he started laughing as well. We stood there holding each other and laughing hysterically. We must have looked like absolute idiots.

"Hey there, lovebirds! We need to start heading up the hill, or I'm going to starve to death standing here watching you two laugh like love-sick puppies," Giselle said, laughing.

I looked over at Ginger, and we both rolled our eyes, smiling.

"Yes, ma'am." Rowan saluted Giselle, who rolled her eyes in response.

Everyone started walking up the hill. Most people walked with their individual families. However, everyone still seemed connected. It was a much happier scene than I'd ever witnessed within my own extended human family.

Except, of course, for Delilah. She was marching up the hill looking as determined as ever, pretending like the rest of us didn't exist. Several times she tripped, almost falling over. Each time, I had to stop myself from laughing. I knew why she didn't like me, but I couldn't imagine why she seemed to despise everyone else, excluding Rowan, just as much. No one attempted to talk to her, so I assumed her behavior must have been normal.

Rowan held my hand as we climbed the hill. He smiled widely, seemingly lost in thought. With almost anyone else, it would have been an awkward silence. Not with Rowan, though. We were content just to be near each other. I smiled to myself, glad that my presence was enough to make Rowan look as if he was the happiest man on Earth.

Everyone went into the meadow, separating into different groups. Rowan went to play football with Colton, Carson, and Cameron. Thomas Smith, Clay Marshall, and Daniel Norris also went to play with them. Forest Jones, William Wood, Anthony Lincoln, Abraham Banks, and Issac Crane all decided to watch the game. The rest of us, excluding

Delilah, went to sit on a blanket nearby. We started unpacking the picnic baskets and organizing the food. Tiffany sat with Lizzy on her lap. She had already fallen asleep, holding on tightly to a fuzzy blue stuffed rabbit. Tiffany was gently rocking her, humming a soft lullaby. Conversation quickly drifted to Eleanor, who was due to deliver in three days.

"I'm always just so hungry. I feel like I could eat all the food in the world, and it still wouldn't be enough." Eleanor rubbed her belly, gazing at a plate of pork chops.

"I had the same problem when I was pregnant with you," her mother said. "I never could get enough to eat. I used to get up in the middle of the night to eat another plate of whatever we had for dinner."

"I never had that problem. Except for pickles. I always wanted more pickles," Marie commented.

"Of course, you know that you're all invited to the party after the baby is born. You too, Lily." Eleanor smiled at me while simultaneously cutting a pork chop.

I smiled back. "Have you picked a name yet?"

"Well, we don't know if it's a boy or a girl. But so far, our choices are Stephanie and Casper. Personally, I hope it's a girl. I can't stand the name Casper, but Daniel is in love with it." She finished the first pork chop and reached to pick up a second one.

"It'll be a girl," Eva said. "We haven't had a boy born into this family for four generations."

"Momma, you know that's just a coincidence. Gender has nothing to do with the mom's side of the family," Eleanor said while chewing.

"I don't believe those scientists for one minute! My grandma always said it was the woman's side." Eva spoke as if it were her lifelong crusade.

Eleanor rolled her eyes while I suppressed a laugh. Looking around, it seemed like everyone else was doing the same.

There was a large crash from over where the game was being played, and we all turned our heads to look. There was lots of yelling, but the only thing I was able to make out was someone shouting, "Old man." Thomas and Carson were playfully wrestling while everyone else appeared to be picking sides. We all laughed, turning to watch the match. Rowan was leaning against a tree a few feet away from them. He was laughing and cheering one of them on. But there was so much yelling that I couldn't tell who he was encouraging.

I turned to my right to ask Ginger if she knew where the ketchup was when I noticed Delilah lying out on the grass near the lake. She had somehow gotten rid of her clothes and was wearing only a bikini—a very small, black bikini. Everyone else was fully clothed, but of course, she couldn't just be normal like the rest of us. I rolled my eyes, feeling more than annoyed. I took a deep breath, trying to calm down.

Ginger had evidently followed my line of sight and was tapping me on the shoulder. "Hey, don't let the witch ruin your day." She smiled, handing me a large sugar cookie.

"Thanks," I muttered.

A little while later, after much more talk about male baby names that were superior to Casper, everyone came over to rest. Rowan walked over and sat between Marie and me. He put his arm around me and kissed my cheek before reaching for a plate. Everyone was occupied with their own conversations and passing the food around. Rowan was piling a mountain of green beans onto his plate with one hand

and eating an apple with the other. I reached for the bowl of grapes and put a handful on my plate.

I heard someone walk up behind me and turned around to see who it was. Rowan evidently heard it, too, because he turned around at the same time. He still had the apple in his mouth, which I thought was adorable. Delilah was standing behind us, her hands on her hips. She had put a pink swim cover up over her bikini. The only problem was that it was see-through. So her tiny black bikini, which barely qualified as clothing, was still entirely visible.

"Ugh." She looked at the apple in Rowan's mouth as if it caused him to instantly turn from a handsome prince into a disgusting caveman. "I see that her adorable quirks have been rubbing off on you," Delilah said as she scrunched her nose as if she were smelling a pair of old, moldy socks.

Ginger noticed Delilah and turned around. "Back off, Delilah." Ginger frowned something that was very out of character.

Delilah laughed, throwing her hands up in the air. "So, the redhead speaks! I wasn't aware that she was capable of uttering anything except gibberish." Delilah grinned, looking directly at Ginger.

Ginger didn't even look upset, obviously accustomed to the comments.

"Go away, Delilah." Rowan had taken the apple out of his mouth, looking as serious as ever. He had a glint of anger in his eyes, which was something I had only seen a few times before.

She smiled a deathly grin at Rowan. I didn't know how one facial expression could be so beautiful and terrifying in equal measure. It was almost like gazing into the eyes of a tiger before it devoured you. She walked away, going to sit by her dad. Thankfully, he was a good distance away from us.

Marie looked at me and reached out to take my hand. "Don't judge her too harshly, Lily. She lost her mother in a terrible car accident when she was only eight. I don't think she's been truly happy since it happened. I know she can be hard to handle at times, but she doesn't mean any real harm. She would never hurt you or any of us." Marie smiled gently at me.

I wanted to believe her. I wanted to believe that there was good in all people. Just a few days ago, I'd even felt sorry for Delilah. Unfortunately, I found it hard to find the good in her when I was positive that she would murder me in an instant if it meant she could be with Rowan. She was like a bad case of acne that would never ever go away.

Rowan put his hand on my back, softly rubbing it. "I'm sorry." He reached out to pull a small piece of hair out from behind my ear.

"It's not your fault. You shouldn't have to apologize for her," I said.

"Ah, but I have to," he whispered. "If I wasn't over here busy apologizing for her, I'd be far too tempted to go over there and punch her perfect, evil face."

I laughed loudly, and several people glanced in our direction. "But you can't," I whispered.

"Why not?" he asked.

"Because, my love, you would have to get in line. You see, I've already reserved 'punching Delilah's perfect, evil face' for the next ten years." I grinned, trying not to laugh.

"This is why I love you." He leaned forward and kissed me.

When he pulled away, my eyes caught Delilah's. She was staring at me with an intensity far darker than I'd ever seen before. I almost thought that I could see tiny lightning bolts flashing behind her eyes.

Chapter 17
Baby

Eleanor had the baby early Tuesday morning, which was a day early. As soon as we got out of school, Rowan and I rushed to her house to see the baby. She'd had a home birth with no complications. Everyone told her that we could wait a few days to see the baby, but she was insistent that we come on Tuesday. Marie and Eva had been there all day helping with the baby and getting ready for the party.

We pulled into the driveway at Eleanor and Daniel's, got out of the car, and walked toward their house, a small grey Craftsman. It had a large front porch, which was currently covered in pink balloons.

"How much do you want to bet that Ginger and Giselle are already here?" Rowan asked.

He poked one of the balloons, and it spun around to show in large, glittery letters, "It's a girl!"

"A kiss?" I raised my eyebrows, grinning at him.

"Deal." He walked over to the front door and knocked.

Marie opened the front door, smiling even brighter than usual.

"Hello! Everyone's already inside," she said. Looking directly at me, she added, "Ginger and Giselle are over by the food."

"Of course they are," I said.

Marie and I shared a quick smile and walked inside.

"You owe me a kiss," Rowan whispered in my ear.

"I'll keep that in mind." I winked at him.

The entire house looked as if it had been hit by a tornado—a tornado containing pink balloons, confetti, and glitter. The tiny living room was practically stuffed full of people. Eleanor was sitting on the couch holding the baby. Daniel was to her right, looking as if he had been through a real tornado. His shirt was buttoned in the wrong holes, he was wearing one long sock and one short sock, and he was wearily rubbing his eyes. Eva was sitting on Eleanor's left side, looking very proud of herself.

"I knew it would be a girl!" she said to no one in particular.

I saw Eleanor roll her eyes. She looked surprisingly well put together, considering she'd given birth fourteen hours ago. She was wearing leggings with a long, yellow maternity blouse. Her hair was pulled back in a professional-looking ponytail, and her makeup was done to perfection. I thought she looked kind of like Cleopatra. Charlotte, William, and Issac were drinking punch in the corner of the room. They seemed to be discussing something about the weather and how it hadn't rained in two weeks. Anthony and Caroline were sitting on the floor, building a castle out of blocks with Lizzy. Looking out the sliding glass doors, I saw that Clay and Thomas were playing a game of soccer with Colton, Carson, and Cameron. Victoria and Tiffany were carrying plates of hamburgers from the grill into the house and placing them on the food table in the corner of the room. Ginger was making a new bowl of punch, while Giselle was trying to do something artistic with the cheese and crackers tray. It looked a bit like the Eiffel Tower, until it fell down. Abraham and Forest were standing along the wall eating hamburgers. Delilah was sitting in an armchair, applying what looked like yet another layer of dark-red lipstick.

"I just love babies!" Marie smiled to herself, obviously remembering when Ginger and Giselle had been little.

"Me too," Rowan said.

I was a little surprised. I hadn't known he'd felt one way or another about them. We'd never really discussed our feelings about having kids. I knew that I wanted several, but I hadn't expected him to feel the same way. We walked over to Eleanor and the baby.

"Congratulations! She's beautiful," I said.

I hadn't been lying either. The baby really was beautiful. She already had a full head of black, curly hair and big brown eyes.

"Thank you. Her name is Stephanie." Eleanor held her up so that I could look at her more closely. Even though I didn't have any siblings, I had four cousins who were significantly younger than me, so I knew how to handle babies. I gently touched her cheek, feeling her soft, fragile skin. She wrapped her little hand around my finger.

"Can I hold her?" Rowan asked.

He had a longing on his face as he looked at Stephanie. He must have really meant it when he said he loved babies.

"Of course," Eleanor said.

She handed Stephanie to Rowan, laying her gently in his arms. He cradled her, rocking her softly. He carried her over to a chair by the unlit fireplace and slowly sat down. I stood beside him, watching how he never let his eyes leave her tiny face. She smiled up at him, snuggling her face against his chest.

"Lily, we should have bunches of kids. I mean bunches," he said, not taking his eyes off the baby in his arms.

I smiled, putting my hand on his back.

"Ha! You'd be lucky if you had one baby that survived," Delilah said, examining her nails. She had a smug look on her face that radiated a sense of superiority.

"Delilah!" Marie said, almost dropping her plate.

"It's true," she said.

Ginger and Giselle had walked over to stand beside me as the room went deadly quiet. The only noise that could be heard was the sound of the soccer game still going on outside. Rowan had gone rigid, his eyes practically burning with fury. Saying I was extremely confused would have been a drastic understatement.

I looked around the room. "Can someone please explain to me what that's supposed to mean?"

Marie's shock quickly turned to panic. "Nothing, honey—"

"There's no reason to lie to her. She'll have to be told eventually," Rowan said.

Somehow Ginger, Giselle, and Marie had become even more pale than usual. Eleanor looked as if she might throw up. Victoria and Tiffany had frozen halfway between the grill and food table, still holding plates full of hamburgers in their hands. Charlotte, who was still playing with Lizzy, took her hand and led her into the backyard. Delilah was reclining in her chair, smirking.

"There is a group of fae, more of a cult really, that doesn't believe humans and faeries should ever be more than friends. They don't think the two should ever mix in terms of romantic relationships," Ginger said, still as pale as a ghost.

"They consider it their personal responsibility to try to prevent marriages between the two," Giselle added, nervously wringing her hands.

"Why?" I asked.

"They think that if too many faeries and humans marry and have children, which are called demi-fae, eventually there won't be any more faeries. They say it's because they don't want faerie magic to disappear." Ginger looked at me sympathetically.

Delilah looked directly at me. "The juicy bit that these two left out is that if the watchers, which is what they're called, come across a human and faerie who are in a relationship, they go to whatever lengths necessary to end the relationship. If all of their other methods fail, they kill the human. Same thing happens if they come across a demi-fae. They kill the baby and the human parent."

I stood there staring at her, my face an emotionless mask. I was too shocked to be upset.

"They aren't common around here, Lily. None of us have ever even met a watcher," Marie said.

Everyone was either staring at the floor or acting as if the food on their plate was the most interesting thing they'd ever seen. Delilah was grinning like it was Christmas and her birthday all wrapped into one.

"Rowan, can I please talk to you alone?" I pulled him up from the chair, and he quickly handed Stephanie back to Eleanor.

I led him into the nearest room, which happened to be Stephanie's nursery and closed the door behind us.

"You never thought of telling me this?" I was frustrated, maybe even angry with Rowan. We'd never had a reason to argue before now, but this was serious. He couldn't just keep life-threatening secrets from me and expect me not to get mad.

"I wanted to tell you, Lily, I really did. I just didn't know what to say. I told you there were dangerous things in my world. I warned you that it wouldn't be an easy way to live."

After looking down, I realized I was standing on something and looked down to see that there was a stuffed unicorn under my left foot. As I reached to pick it up, my fingers grazed its soft fur. My eyes traced the room. The walls were painted a light shade of purple. The floor was a soft, cream colored carpet. There was a white crib on the far wall and a tall lamp beside it. There was also a changing table with large, light-up letters above it that spelled Stephanie's name. Toys were scattered around the floor, and a cushioned rocking chair sat in the corner of the room. It was ironic. We were standing in a nursery discussing the people who would want to kill both me and any future children we might have.

I set the unicorn down inside the crib and turned around to look at him. He was running his hands through his hair, staring at the floor. He did look sorry. I couldn't bring myself to be angry with him for long.

"Rowan, I'm not angry. But this isn't about either of us." I gestured to the crib. Rowan looked at it, obviously understanding my meaning. "It's about them, our future children. I don't care about the danger to myself, but I can't bear the thought of subjecting them to a lifetime of fear." I covered my face with my hands, feeling the tears falling down my cheeks.

As much as I hated the idea of forcing my children to live in the shadows, I couldn't deny Rowan the opportunity to have them. The way he'd held Stephanie looked so natural. He was one of those people you could tell was born to be a parent. And I wanted them too. I wanted to see babies who were half of me and half of the man I loved. I wanted to share my favorite books with them, to watch them play in the meadow, to see them learn how to use the abilities that their faerie lineage would give them.

Rowan pulled me into his arms. My tears fell harder, soaking into the fabric of his shirt. He held me there for a long time, rubbing my back. I leaned over and buried my face in his shirt, the same way Stephanie had done earlier. He only wrapped his arms tighter around me and let me cry. Finally, the tears stopped falling.

"Lily, you know I'd never let anyone hurt you. I know you said you don't care about your safety, but I do. I care about you just as much as any of the possible children we might have. So if you don't want to have any, to protect them, I understand."

Rowan let go of me. I looked up at him and could see the pain in his eyes. I couldn't deny him what he obviously so desperately wanted.

"No, Rowan, I want to have them. We'll worry about how to protect them when it becomes an issue. Marie said the watchers were rare, so maybe we'll never even have to worry about it." I tried to give him a reassuring smile.

"Yeah, maybe," he said.

I could hear the doubt in his voice.

We went back into the living room, where it appeared that the entire incident had been forgotten. Everyone was talking excitedly about something, but I couldn't figure out what it was.

"Oh, Lily, Rowan, come here!" Giselle squealed, bouncing up and down.

We walked over as Rowan slipped his hand in mine.

Ginger, Giselle, and Marie, were all crowded around Eleanor, who was holding Stephanie.

"Look, you can see little flames in her hand!" Ginger whispered, very excitedly.

I looked down at Stephanie, who was indeed producing small sparks out of her palm. Seeing a newborn baby holding fire in their hand would alarm the average person, but I'd gotten so accustomed to Rowan shooting beams of light that it didn't even seem strange to me.

"She's a fire faerie!" Giselle was practically bursting with excitement.

Rowan and I grinned at each other. "You still owe me that kiss," he grinned.

"How could I forget?" I leaned forward and kissed him.

I was fully aware that Delilah was glaring at me from the corner of the room, and I couldn't have cared less.

Chapter 18
The Sleepover

On Friday, I spent the night at Ginger and Giselle's house. I remembered thinking I didn't know much about their personal lives, and decided this was a good opportunity to learn more about them. After dinner we went upstairs to their room, taking lots of snacks with us. Marie literally made the best cookies I had ever tasted, and I wasn't going to lose this opportunity to eat a plate full of them. We changed into more comfortable clothes and removed all of our makeup. This took Ginger and Giselle significantly longer than it took me, since I was only wearing a little mascara, while they were wearing full faces of makeup. Ginger and Giselle both sat on bean bags while I sat in the fluffy pink chair. I recalled that we were sitting in the same places we had sat on the day I met them. It was strange, considering that when I met them, I would have never guessed that we'd end up being best friends.

"So, Ginger, tell me about your fiancé." I took a large bite out of a sugar cookie, chewing quietly.

"Well, his name is Drew Green, and he's blond — like, really blond. His hair is actually closer to white. But it's real. Don't worry, I wouldn't marry a guy who bleached his hair." She grinned, playing with one of the curls falling around her face.

"Eww," Giselle and I said at the same time.

We all started laughing. Giselle laughed so hard that

she fell backwards, which only made us all laugh harder.

"Okay, okay. Where does he work?" I asked.

"Oooh, he's a police officer in the NYPD!" Giselle squealed.

"Ooh." I grinned at Ginger. Her face was bright red, and she was giggling.

"How old is he?" I asked.

"He's twenty-one," Ginger said, blushing even more.

"Two years older? He's practically ancient!" I laughed.

Giselle roared with laughter while Ginger playfully threw a pink teddy bear at me. I caught the teddy bear, causing her to playfully stick her tongue out at me.

"Is he a fire fairy too, or something different?" I asked.

"He's human. I waited until we'd been seeing each other for about six months before I told him I was a faerie. He thought I was joking until I picked a candle up and a flame erupted from its wick," Ginger said.

"I was there when she told him. You should have seen the look on his face! He looked terrified at first, but then he got down on one knee and proposed." Giselle stared lovingly at the ceiling as if waiting for her prince to ride in on a white horse and whisk her away.

"That's really romantic," I said.

"I know," Ginger sighed.

"Yeah, but you two are lucky!" Giselle exclaimed. "You've both already found perfect partners. I haven't been on a single successful date in my life! What if I get old and ugly before I can find a handsome brunette to run away with to some tropical island?" She threw her hands up in the air.

"You're only nineteen. You have at least five more years before you become a hopeless spinster," I laughed.

"Drama queen," Ginger said to Giselle, smirking.

This led to a full-blown battle between Ginger and Giselle, who began hurling pillows and stuffed animals at each other. We were all laughing hysterically. As soon as a large, green turtle landed in my lap, I joined in on the fight. The room soon became a war zone as we ducked behind beds and chairs to avoid being hit, while throwing the objects aimed at us back in the direction they had come from. As strange as it seemed, I didn't think I'd ever had as much fun in my life.

Eventually, we called a truce. We decided to watch a movie before going to bed. I recommended *Sense and Sensibility*, which Ginger and Giselle had never seen or read before. By the end of the movie, Giselle was ugly-crying, holding a wad of used tissues in her hand. Similarly, Ginger was biting her nails, staring intently at the screen. I smiled, watching the final scene of the movie with the kind of fondness that one might watch a video of a childhood friend. I'd watched the movie so many times that it was more of a comfort to me than a heart-wrenching romance.

We turned the TV off and crawled into the sleeping bags we'd placed on the floor. I tried to fall asleep, but my mind kept returning to the conversation we'd had earlier that evening. About thirty minutes later, I gave up trying to fall asleep. I could hear Giselle snoring beside me. I rolled over on my right side, facing Ginger.

"Ginger, are you awake?" I whispered.

"Yes." She opened her eyes, looking at me.

"How did you meet Drew?" I asked.

She smiled. "His aunt is one of my mom's friends. He was here visiting with his family over the summer, and his aunt invited us all over to her house to meet them. We became friends first, but we both started having feelings for each other within a couple of months."

"Are you worried about the watchers because he's human?" I asked.

I knew it was wrong, but I was glad he was human simply because I'd have someone to share my fears with.

"Yeah, I am, but Delilah didn't make such a big show about it when I told everyone that I was dating a human," she whispered.

"Do you think it was just out of spite because of her jealousy?" I asked.

"Yeah, she probably just wanted to get under your skin. I've only ever heard of watchers attacking high profile faeries who were practically advertising what they were and that they were in a relationship with a human. I doubt that there's much to worry about, especially since we've got a good support system of reliable faeries who would risk their own lives to protect us. You're part of our family now too, Lily." Ginger reached out and squeezed my hand.

"I'm glad," I whispered.

She smiled at me and closed her eyes to go to sleep. I could still hear Giselle snoring, though not as loudly as before. I closed my eyes, determined to put all thoughts of the watchers out of my mind as I fell asleep between my two best friends.

Chapter 19
The Fight

We slept in a little the next morning, but since Rowan was supposed to pick me up for lunch around noon, I had to get home. Ginger and Giselle dropped me off at my house, promising that we'd have another sleepover soon. I didn't expect my parents to be home. Saturday was usually a busy day for the store since lots of people were off work. Slipping the key out of my pocket, I unlocked the front door and went inside. Since I was in a bit of a rush, I left my backpack and overnight bag by the door and went up to my room to grab a jacket. It was a little cold outside, and the shirt I'd packed to wear today wasn't warm enough. Without having a moment to think, I opened the door to my room and screamed.

Jack was sitting on the edge of my bed, crying. He looked up at me, his eyes puffy and red. He looked like he hadn't slept in weeks.

"Jack, what are you doing in my room? And why are you crying?" I asked.

"Lily, I'm so sorry. I tried to stop this, I really did, but you wouldn't listen to me." Jack looked back down at the floor, his hand balled into tight fists.

"Stop what?" I asked. "Jack, is this about the drinking?"

"No, Lily, this is about you and Rowan. About you refusing to give him up no matter how many times I asked you to." Jack ran his hands through his hair, tugging and ripping small parts out.

"Jack, I know about your feelings for me. I just don't feel the same way about you. I'm sorry." I started walking toward him, but he put his hand out to stop me.

"I've always loved you, Lily, from the moment I ran into you and knocked you over at freshman orientation. And I still love you. But just as I knew from the moment I started loving you, I still know that you can never be mine. But that's not what any of this is about. I'm a faerie, Lily, like Rowan is. My parents are watchers. That's why I knew I could never be more than a friend to you. And I was prepared for that. I was prepared for you to fall in love with a human man and have a family with him, completely oblivious to my feelings for you. My parents were even all right with it as long as I never told you what I was or how I felt about you. Everything was fine until you became involved with him." Jack said the word "him" like it was a curse. "Rowan ruined everything. He made you fall in love with him before I could convince you to stay away from him. They gave me months, Lily, months to talk you out of being with him. But now my time is up. My parents told me they would do it so I wouldn't have to watch it happen. They promised that it would be painless, that you wouldn't feel a thing. I did everything I could to make myself forget you. I drank, smoked, anything to keep my mind off you. But it never worked. You were always on my mind, a constant presence in my thoughts. I just couldn't stand the thought of you dying and me not being here. I was planning on doing it myself, quietly while you slept. I didn't want you to feel any pain. Then she came and—"

"Shut up, Jack. You asked for time to give her an explanation, but time's up." Delilah stepped into the room, standing between me and the door. "Now it's my turn." She grinned in the most menacing, evil way I could have imagined. Small bursts of lightning were coming from Delilah's palms as she started walking toward me. Jack was lying on my bed now, screaming more than crying.

My mind raced. I tried to think of anything around me that I could use for a weapon. I knew that my best option was to hide until Rowan got there, but I had to have a way to defend myself until I could find a hiding spot. If I could make Delilah move from in front of the door, I might be able to run fast enough to get out of the room. I grabbed a stack of hardcover books off my shelf and started throwing them at Delilah while running toward the door. It seemed to annoy her more than hurt her, but it didn't matter as long as it distracted her. I would be forever grateful for spending the extra money on hardcover books rather than paperbacks.

I ran down the stairs and into the kitchen as fast as I could. I could hear Delilah screaming at Jack to stop crying and start helping her. I grabbed a large frying pan and a large knife before hiding in the pantry. I shut the door behind me and immediately took my phone out of my back pocket. I couldn't exactly call nine-one-one and tell them that my faerie boyfriend's psycho ex-girlfriend, who was apparently part of some prejudiced faerie cult, was trying to murder me by shooting lightning out of her hands. They'd probably just tell me to check myself into the mental ward at the hospital. Rowan was already on his way, but I sent him a text updating him on the situation. I also sent messages to Ginger and Giselle, asking them to bring whatever help they could.

I put my phone back in my pocket and attempted to hide behind a large bag of rice. I held the knife with my right hand, pointing it toward the pantry door. I heard footsteps on the stairs and tried to quiet my breathing.

Delilah started talking. "I know you're here somewhere, Lily. It's only a matter of time before I find you. Do you know why I want to kill you? You probably think you do, but you're wrong. Neither I nor my family are watchers. I was just lucky enough to overhear your redhead besties talking about your miserable little love triangle. I decided that I would find this Jack person and make a deal with him. If he helped me ruin your relationship with Rowan, then we would both get what we wanted. He could finally be with you, and I could be with Rowan. But when I finally found him, I realized I'd come across a family of watchers. Of course, he doesn't call himself one yet, but he will eventually. I was thrilled to find that he'd already been given the task of killing you. Unfortunately, he was planning on doing it painlessly, which I would not agree to. So I simply told him I was going to come here and kill you myself today, with or without him. As you can see, he decided to come along. Of course, I've now realized that his help is absolutely useless. He doesn't seem to have much of a tendency toward aggression. But none of that is what's important. What's important is that you've attempted to steal what's mine. My mother told me from the moment we were born that Rowan and I were destined to be together. When she was still alive, she used to tell me how she and Rowan's mom, who was her best friend, had talked about how their children would fall in love. They'd talked about our wedding, how many children we would have, and even what type of house we'd live in. It was their dream for their children to marry. So you see, Lily, he was mine all along. He was promised to me!"

At that moment, my phone started ringing.

Before I even had time to panic, the pantry door was flung open. Like any person would, I acted instinctively, standing up and lunging forward. The knife went into her right shoulder, causing her to scream. The knife fell from my hands as I ran behind her. With all the force I was capable of, I swung the frying pan, hitting the right side of her face. She screamed louder, tugging the knife out of her shoulder to reveal a mess of butchered flesh. She aimed the knife, now drenched in blood, at me. With terror beating through my heart, I sprinted out the front door, running into Jack, who was standing on the porch. We both fell over, landing beside each other. He started to sit up, but I hit him with the frying pan, knocking him out. In all honesty, I had no idea that I could hit that hard.

Delilah burst out the front door, blood still dripping from her shoulder. She glanced down at Jack, unconscious on the porch, and screamed. She kicked his unconscious form, still screaming. I couldn't tell whether she was screaming out of frustration or pain.

I stood up, backing into one of my pots of plants. My fingers grazed the leaf of a sage plant. I felt a sudden tingling in my fingers, which quickly extended throughout my body. Delilah approached me, knife in hand. Something inside me seemed to tell me to wrap my hands around the stem of the plant. I followed my intuition and willed whatever was going to happen to happen quickly.

In a moment of absolute amazement, I felt a burst of energy, both physical and mental, escape my body. The energy flowed through my fingers and into the plant. The stem started to grow in size and was soon large enough to pass for a small tree. Without making a conscious choice to move, I stepped back, staring at the plant in shock. My hand was shaking uncontrollably. I honestly couldn't believe what I was seeing. The plant placed itself like a wall between Delilah and I. She dropped the knife, staring in horror, her mouth wide open.

I heard running footsteps and looked toward the driveway. Rowan was sprinting toward the porch with an expression of pure terror on his face. Two more cars pulled into the driveway. I could hear another car racing down the street. Delilah took one look at Rowan and ran. She jumped off the side of the porch and dashed into the woods behind my house. Jack was still unconscious.

The plant started to angle itself between Rowan and me. He stared at me from the steps of the porch, looking as if he'd seen a ghost. The same instinct that had led me to touch the plant before directed me to touch it again. I placed my hands on the plant, directing my energy toward it. This time I paid more attention to the sensation flowing through my body. The action itself was draining, like running a marathon without any conditioning. If I concentrated hard enough, I could understand the plant communicating with me during the energy change. It was almost as if it could understand my thoughts. The plant shrank back to its original size just as quickly as it had originally grown. I looked at my hands, holding them up in front of my face.

Suddenly Rowan was wrapping his arms around me. He picked me up and carried me into the living room. With all the force I had left in my being, I curled my body into him, letting his familiar scent distract me from everything that had just happened. He laid me down on the couch, kneeling beside me. Something within me acknowledged that I could hear people talking outside — comfort coursed through me as I recognized Ginger, Giselle, and Marie's voices. It took all of my energy to turn my head to look out the window. Forest and Clay were standing with them. My head was spinning; the whole room seemed to be going in and out of focus. Rowan was looking at me with astonishment and fear equally displayed on his face. He whispered soft, reassuring phrases in my ear. I didn't think I had enough energy to process anything else, but then I heard Jack's voice. Jack ran into the room, Forest and Clay right behind him. Forest grabbed both of Jack's arms and held them behind his back.

"Lily! Please, just let me say one more thing to you. Please! I'll leave you alone for the rest of your life if you'll just give me the chance to talk to you. Please!" Jack's eyes pleaded with me, begging me to let him speak.

Forest looked to me as if asking for my permission to let Jack talk. I nodded.

"What I said to you earlier was true! I love you! I've always loved you! I was wrong to try to hurt you. I don't believe the same things as my parents. You and I, we were made for each other! We can run away right now, just you and me. We can have a life together! Please, Lily, I love you!"

"Liar!" Rowan roared. "You didn't try to hurt her, you tried to kill her! You're a filthy watcher, just like your parents!"

Rowan was standing up now, his hands balled into fists. I still felt like the room was spinning a hundred miles an hour.

"Lily, please, come with me," Jack spoke so quietly that I could barely hear what he'd said.

"She's not going anywhere with you ever again!"

Rowan's fists were shaking like they couldn't wait to be put to good use.

"That is her decision, not yours!" Jack yelled.

Forest tightened his grip on Jack's arms, causing Jack to wince in pain. Clay had found a rope somewhere and was beginning to tie it around Jack's wrists.

"Lily, please." Tears were now falling down Jack's cheeks.

I took a deep breath, realizing that I was crying too. Rowan was staring at Jack with what looked like pure hatred in his eyes. Jack was only looking at me.

"The Jack that I knew is gone." I turned my head away from him, closing my eyes.

It was impossible to ignore the tears falling down my cheeks. My body was shaking, and I could barely breathe. Rowan knelt back down beside me, taking my hands in his. He pushed my hair out of my face, which was now drenched in layers of sweat. There was something within my chest urging me not to look at Jack. In all honesty, I was afraid that if I did, I wouldn't ever be able to look away again.

"You have precisely twenty-four hours to collect your things and leave," Forest said. "You are *never* to try to contact Lily again. If you do attempt to contact them or do not leave within twenty-four hours, you'll be seeing us again."

I heard the front door open and close. Jack was gone, and I knew that a not-so-small part of me was gone with him.

I felt Rowan pick me up off of the couch and carry me upstairs. His muscles were tense, filled with unused rage. He laid me down on the bed and pulled a chair over to sit beside me. He held my hand, gently stroking my thumb with his. I felt the tears drying on my cheeks and mixing with the already dried sweat. The room went fuzzy, even more so than before. Colors no longer seemed to exist as the room turned into a sea of white, grey, and black. The edges of my vision disappeared. Everything was fading away. The pain in my head slowly became a gentle pull toward sleep. Then I gave into the darkness.

Chapter 20
THE DISCOVERY

I knew I was awake when I realized I was holding someone's hand. Or, more likely, they were holding my hand while I slept. As much I wished it wasn't the case, I had no problem remembering what had happened earlier. The knowledge had stayed with me through my dreamless sleep and was still there, ready to hit my heart like a brick when I woke up. Considering myself rather clever, I contemplated pretending to still be asleep. Like any normal person would in my situation, I wanted to pull the covers up over my head and stay safely tucked away in my warm, fuzzy blankets. But I knew that the discovery I had made earlier wasn't simply going to disappear, even if I did go back to sleep. There was no way I could ignore my new reality. I was a faerie, or at least part faerie. After what had happened with my sage plant, there was no denying the truth of the statement.

Pulling me away from my thoughts, I felt the hand that I was holding gently tighten. My eyes opened to see that Rowan was in the same place he had been when I'd fallen asleep. The difference was that he was now sleeping while I was awake. It was fascinating that I could tell that he was dreaming. His eyes were moving slightly underneath his eyelids, and he was deeply frowning. A book titled *Clockwork Princess* lay open on his lap. Despite recent events, I was still the bookworm I had been before. My curiosity got the best of me, and I leaned over to glance at the page number. He was on page twenty. I noticed that there were two piles of books on the floor beside his chair. *Clockwork Angel* and *Clockwork Prince* made up the first stack. *The Call of The Wild, Frankenstein*, and *Of Mice and Men* were in the second stack. It was a unique assortment of books, but then again, Rowan was a unique person. I knew that the books weren't mine and wondered why he would have brought so many with him.

Glancing over, I then saw the pile of flowers, chocolate, and cards stacked beside my bed. Slowly I opened the first card; it was from Ginger and Giselle. Looking back at Rowan, I realized he was wearing different clothes than he had been when he'd carried me upstairs. I glanced back down at the floor and noticed a duffle bag behind Rowan's chair. The clothes he'd worn before were scrunched up into a ball in the bag. There was *no* way that I'd slept for a whole day. Quickly I grabbed my phone from my nightstand and looked at the date. It was Sunday morning. It was almost unbelievable—I had slept through the rest of the day and all night. Everyone who knew about the incident had evidently sent cards and other comforting items. Apparently, someone had also thought to bring Rowan a change of clothes, along with some books to occupy his time. As reality began to set in on me, I sincerely hoped they'd figured out a convincing explanation to tell my parents.

Rowan opened his eyes and immediately looked at me. He seemed surprised that he'd fallen asleep. He took the book off his lap and placed it in the first pile on the floor. He leaned closer to me, softly smiling.

"Hey, I'm sorry I fell asleep," he said, gently stroking my face with his fingers.

"Don't apologize, you need sleep too," I said, reaching up to hold his hand in mine. He pulled my hand over to his lips and kissed it.

"I wanted to be here when you woke up. Ginger and Giselle put up a bit of a protest, saying they wanted to stay with you, but I ended up winning." He grinned at me, but it didn't reach his eyes. They looked as if they had been taken out and replaced with a much older pair that had seen more than their fair share of horrors.

"Are we going to talk about it?" I asked.

I pulled myself up into a sitting position. Quickly glancing at my nightstand, I located a hair-clip. I pulled my hair up into a large bun on the top of my head and looked back at Rowan. His usual expressions of either amusement or happiness were not present on his face.

"Which part did you want to talk about?" he asked. His voice seemed hollow, devoid of any emotion.

"Well, there's not much to talk about in terms of Jack," I said. My voice was a little unsteady, but I managed to keep myself from becoming over emotional. "I don't know what happened to Delilah, but she seemed to be bleeding pretty badly when she ran away." I looked at Rowan, attempting to decipher his blank expression.

"She's gone. No one saw her after she ran, but her dad has left town, along with all of their stuff. Clay went by his house this morning to tell him what happened, but except for a few pieces of furniture, the house was empty."

His expression was still as blank as an unused piece of paper. He looked down at the floor, suddenly very interested in the carpet. It was obvious that he was avoiding eye contact with me. I didn't understand why.

"All right, so let's talk about me. I'm obviously a faerie; no human could have done what I did with the sage plant," I said.

Rowan looked up at me. His face was no longer emotionless but instead displayed a deep, uncontrollable sadness.

Then it hit me. For a second, time seemed to stand still. My breathing froze, and even my heart seemed to stop beating. The only thing functioning in my body were the wheels in my brain, which were turning unbelievably fast. If I was a faerie or even a demi-fae, it was impossible for me to have two human parents. My parents *weren't* my parents. Thousands of possibilities flooded my brain. Had my mom cheated on my dad? Was I adopted? Was I the product of a horrible crime committed against my mother? Had I been accidentally switched at birth? Had I been intentionally exchanged with another baby? My brain kept turning, spinning, the possibilities swimming through my mind.

Rowan touched my shoulders. "Lily, breathe."

In very Lily-like fashion, I had been holding my breath without even realizing it. When my throat began to beg for oxygen, I took a deep breath, rubbing my forehead. He looked at me nervously, as if trying to decide if I was going to start throwing things across the room or cry. Honestly, I didn't know what I was going to do either. There was frustration bubbling up within me, but I didn't think I was angry in an aggressive way; it was more of a cold anger. The type of anger that led people to seek revenge years after they had been wronged. It was absolutely bizarre since I'd never felt that type of emotion before. There was also a certain sadness mixed in with my anger, but it wasn't the kind of sadness that caused someone to cry. It was the type of sadness you felt after you had accepted something you didn't want. But I felt it everywhere in my body. For a moment, my inner nerd almost got the best of me. It wanted to examine how my brain was capable of making me feel both extreme anger and sadness simultaneously. It really was incredible.

Despite being both angry and sad, I was also frustrated. Being the type-A personality that I was, I was frustrated with myself for living eighteen years of my life without realizing I wasn't human. There was no doubt in my mind that I was smarter than that. The ironic part was that I'd spent years reading books about characters who discovered they were more than human, not realizing I was too. Denial could do wonders to the brain, human or not. I'd so earnestly believed that those types of things didn't exist that I never even thought to consider the possibility.

Rowan had apparently decided that I was safe to talk to and moved closer to me.

"I suspected it when I first saw you with your garden. The plants seemed to become more vibrant simply from being around you. Of course, it didn't have as much of an effect since you weren't consciously channeling your magic to make them grow. But common sense told me that there was no way a faerie could have two human parents, so I dismissed the idea. I decided that you were simply good at gardening." He softly smiled.

"I'm a summer faerie then?" I asked.

"Doubtful. Most faeries tend to either look or have personality traits that reflect their affinity. You're not blonde or tan. Most summer faeries are also considered to be charming or sociable. You're not exactly a social butterfly. Based on your physical appearance and your dislike of worldly beauty, I'd say that you're an earth faerie. The only other possibility would be spring, but you don't really fit the part. Most spring faeries can work well with both plants and water, but you seem to be limited to plants. But there's also a possibility that you're an earth demi-fae. There's no difference other than that the children of humans and demi-fae are usually born human. They can only produce faerie children with other faeries."

"So there's no way to tell which one I am?" I asked out of pure curiosity.

"No, not unless we knew for sure who your parents were." The carpet suddenly became very interesting to him again.

"Well, lucky for us, that's exactly what I intend to find out."

After getting out of bed, I walked straight to the bathroom. Rowan was watching me with a proud expression on his face. I turned on the shower water and waited for it to warm up. There was simply no question about it—I was going to find out what I was, even if it meant that I had to confront my parents about the secret they'd been keeping from me. I wanted to know not just who but *what* I was, even if it was only for the personal satisfaction of knowing I was able to figure it out.

Chapter 21
THE LETTER

I was in my room after school working on an essay when my parents walked in. Rowan had made sure the house was back in order after the attack before my parents came home. He'd also come up with a very convincing story about my falling down the porch steps, hitting my head, and passing out. He told them that he'd found me unconscious on the sidewalk when he'd come to pick me up for lunch. Considering my natural tendency towards clumsiness, my parents had believed it without any hint of suspicion. It was the first time in my life that I'd been glad that I had no athletic ability.

I hadn't had a chance to talk to them about my questionable parentage yet since they'd been busy working at the store. It was a rare occurrence when both of my parents took time away from work to come and talk to me, especially on a weekday. Whatever they had come to discuss with me today must have been important. From the looks on their faces, whatever they had to tell me must not have only been important, but also bad.

My mom was holding a box, along with an envelope. Her hands were shaking, and her face was filled with dread. My dad was not holding any reading material in his hands, which was shocking in itself. I couldn't remember the last time I'd seen him when he wasn't reading. He took his glasses off, rubbing his face.

"Lily, now that you're about to graduate, there's something your dad and I want to tell you." Mom's voice was shaking violently.

"All right, what is it?" I asked.

They walked toward me. My mom sat on the edge of my bed, placing the box and envelope beside her. My dad stood awkwardly beside the bed, nervously adjusting his glasses.

"Well, after your dad and I got married, we started trying for a baby right away. We already owned the store and were financially stable, so we saw no reason to wait. We tried for around two years before going to a fertility expert. The doctor told us that I wasn't able to have children." She took a deep breath, obviously trying to hold back tears.

My dad was wringing his hands, his eyes moving quickly around the room. If my mom was looking to him for help with her explanation, she wasn't going to get it.

"So after he told us that we couldn't have biological children, we started researching adoption agencies. It took two more years, but we were eventually selected. Your biological mother had chosen us as your adoptive parents. She was eight months pregnant when we found out that you were going to be ours." She handed me the envelope, smiling lightly.

I opened the envelope and found my adoption certificate and some other legal papers. There were several pictures of my parents holding me and the adoption certificate in front of a hospital I didn't recognize. They were absolutely beaming with happiness. In one of the pictures, they were holding me between them, kissing. I didn't think I'd ever seen them that happy before. There were several pictures of me by myself, tightly wrapped in a pink blanket. I'd seen plenty of baby pictures of myself before, but I saw them in a completely different light now.

This was the answer I'd been looking for. I was glad that there was at least a normal explanation. I'd been adopted at birth, the same way that lots of human babies were. But I couldn't help worrying about my biological mother. If she was a faerie, why would she have given me to a human couple to raise? She had to know that I would eventually discover my abilities. There had to be more to this story, but I was pretty sure my parents didn't know anything about it. As far as they knew, they had adopted a normal baby girl who needed a family.

"We wanted to tell you earlier, honey. We were just so afraid that you'd be angry with us." She handed me the box.

It was blue with small, pink flowers scattered across it. It looked as if it had been hand painted by a skilled artist. I took the lid off and placed it on the bed beside me.

"Your biological mother's only request was that we give this box to you when we told you that you were adopted. She asked us not to open it, but simply to give it to you. We'll leave you to look through it." She gave me a quick kiss on the cheek and walked out of the room. My dad quickly smiled at me and followed her.

I began emptying the box, handling each item with care. The first thing I took out was a tiny purple stuffed elephant. It was no larger than my hand, and had obviously been intended to be a baby's toy. I held it briefly, then placed it gently on the bed. Underneath the elephant was an obviously homemade baby hat. It was a rainbow of colors, but predominantly featured green and pink. It looked as if it had been designed to fit the head of a newborn, probably me. I set it down beside the elephant.

With each item I took out of the box I felt that I was uncovering a small part of a past I'd never known I had. The next thing I took out of the box was a small stack of pictures tied together with a ribbon — ultrasound photos. There were pictures of my hands, feet, face, and one of my entire body. My biological mother must have really cared about me to give these pictures up so that I could have them.

There was another stack of pictures in the box. I put the ultrasound ones down and took out the others. They seemed to be from a maternity photoshoot. She was obviously extremely pregnant in the pictures. In truth, she didn't look much older than me. My biological mother was wearing a long sundress with sandals. It was a bit strange to see that she looked very similar to me, with long straight brown hair and pale skin. But her eyes were a light shade of blue rather than green like mine. Looking blissful, she was either laughing or smiling in all of the pictures. In most of them, her hands were placed protectively over her large belly, almost as if she were holding it up.

I noticed two silver rings, one with a large diamond, on her ring finger. She was married. I quickly looked through the rest of the pictures. On the bottom of the stack were three pictures different from the rest. They featured both my biological mother and father. He looked almost nothing like me. He had curly black hair and extremely tan skin. He was also much taller than either myself or my mother. The only trait I appeared to inherit from him was my eyes. His were the same shade of bright, adventurous green as mine. In the three pictures that they were in together, they looked blissful. They were smiling, laughing, and kissing. In one of the pictures, he was on one knee kissing her belly. It was very clear that they were happily in love. I couldn't understand why a young, happy, married couple would ever choose to give up a baby that they seemed to be anxiously waiting for. It didn't make any sense to me.

I put the pictures down and looked back in the box. There was a letter at the bottom in a plain white envelope. I opened it and pulled out a piece of cream-colored stationary with small flowers around the edges.

To my previous baby girl,

The first thing I want you to know is that neither your father or I ever stopped loving you. I know this may seem hard to believe, as this is probably the day you will feel the most alone in your entire life. Although I'm sure that you are very confused, I will try my best to explain everything to you. The easiest way I can think to help you understand is to start at the very beginning.

I met your father, whose name was Joshua Robins, in high school, when we were both sixteen years old. He was very popular and athletic, while I was a shy girl who spent most of my time painting. We were assigned as partners in English class to work on a joint book report. I, who adore reading, was excited to work on the project. However, I was not excited to work with one of the school's most popular boys, who I considered to be extremely immature. I was very wrong. He was not immature, but rather thoughtful and attentive. He was a wonderful, caring friend. Within a few months, we were in love.

This is where I must stop in my narrative to explain a very important aspect of the story itself. I am sure that you are aware by this time that you are very unique. You may have even discovered your abilities by now. The reason you are different is one that you may find very hard to consider factual, but it is something that you must learn to accept. I am a faerie, and as a result of this, you are a half faerie, a demi-fae. I do not know if this knowledge will come as a shock to you or if you have already discovered it on your own. However, my love, you should know that what you are could put you in great danger, which you will come to understand as I continue with my story.

After many months, I finally told your father of my identity. He was shocked at first, but believed me, as I am not the type of person to joke about those sorts of things. He was completely convinced after I showed him the effect that I have on plants. You might be curious to know that I'm an earth faerie. It is possible that you are too, as faerie affinities are sometimes passed from parent to child. Your father was very accepting of my identity. For the next several years, our lives were as normal as they could possibly be. After high school, your father went straight to work as a mechanic while I went to a small college very close to our hometown. I studied art, hoping to become both a professional artist and a high school art teacher.

We got married on New Year's Eve when we were twenty. About a year and a half later, we found out that we were expecting. The baby, of course, was you. For a while, everything was perfect. My pregnancy was devoid of any of the usual problems. I had no morning sickness or swelling. Many people, including your father, remarked that I looked healthier being pregnant than I had before. Unfortunately, that all changed. We were driving home from one of my many doctor's appointments when another car ran directly into us. Your father was killed, instantly. The doctors told me it was a miracle that you and I made it out of the accident alive. I had a *broken wrist, but was otherwise unharmed.*

Very soon after the crash, I found out that it had been orchestrated by a group of faeries known as the watchers. They are a cult that pride themselves on preventing humans and faeries from having relationships. They believe it is their duty to make sure that faerie magic is preserved, and consider demi-fae to be abominations. This is why, my sweet angel, you must make sure to keep yourself safe. Your very existence puts you in harm's way, and for that I am truly sorry. It was very obvious that the crash was intended to kill all three of us, and for this reason I have chosen to give you up. Everyone, apart from your grandma, believes the accident caused your heart to stop beating while still inside me. As far as the world knows, you were not born alive. I have chosen a kind-looking couple from a nearby town, called Oak Valley, to be your adoptive parents. I know there is a decent sized faerie population in that area, and I hope you will reach out to them. They may be able to help you learn more about yourself and what you are capable of. A friend of mine has a cousin who lives in Oak Valley. His name is Forest Jones. Although I have only met him once, I know that he is the type of person who would be willing to help you if you are ever in need of his assistance.

Now that I have explained everything to you, I hope that you will one day be able to forgive me for giving you up. You might like to know that the last thing your father ever did was put his hand on my stomach, intending to protect you from the impact of the crash. I hope it will bring you some comfort to know you were the last thing he ever thought of. He always called you his little angel. The toy elephant I put in the box was one of the many toys he had already filled your nursery with. As for the baby hat, I made it myself. I want you to know that everything I did was to protect you. I will never stop loving you, and will think about you everyday for the rest of my life. You will always be my little princess.

With a heart full of love,

Your mother, Jane Robins

Unable to pull my eyes away, I stared at the letter shocked, horrified, and amazed. The story of my birth was one of selfless love, but also terrible tragedy. My biological father had been killed by the same people who had tried to kill me. Truthfully, I couldn't even imagine how brave my mother must have been to give me up, knowing that she would likely never see me again. The one thing I knew was that I had to find her. She sounded so brave, so mature to have only been twenty-two. I was going to find her and thank her for loving me enough to let me go.

I started to put everything back in the box when I noticed another, far smaller envelope that had been under the letter. After carefully opening it, I found both a picture and a small piece of paper inside. The picture was of my mother and me. She was holding me against her chest, apparently only moments after I had been born. Carefully I put it back inside the envelope. I picked up the piece of paper to read what it said. There was no message or letter; it was simply an address.

With shaking hands, I put everything back in the box except the address and letter from my mother. Then I picked up the phone and called Ginger.

Chapter 22
WHAT FRIENDS ARE FOR

Ginger and Giselle arrived at my house no more than five minutes after I'd called them. Rowan, who happened to be at the library when I'd sent him a text telling him that I needed him, was only about five minutes after them. We sat in my living room, since my parents had left for work and we didn't have to worry about them overhearing us. Rowan was sitting beside me on the couch, reading the letter from my mother. He didn't look happy, to say the least. Ginger, who had already read the letter, was pacing back and forth in the middle of the room. Giselle was trying to Google the address on the second note, wanting to see if she could figure out where it was. Rowan finished reading the letter and handed it back to me. The room was so quiet that the only thing we could hear was each other's breathing.

"I think I should go to the address," I said.

"Well, of course we'll go with you if you do," Ginger said, finally standing still. "The whole thing just seems suspicious to me."

"I agree, it does seem strange," Rowan said.

"The part that bothers me the most is that the handwriting on the address and the letter are drastically different. There's no way that they were written by the same person," Ginger said.

Honestly, I'd never thought about that before. I'd been

so focused on finding my birth mother that I hadn't considered the possibility that she might not have written both notes.

"It could have been planted there by a watcher. They may have discovered that you weren't killed in the crash, but didn't know a way to locate you immediately. They wanted to make sure that if you ever discovered what you were, they would be able to get rid of you," Rowan said. His voice was grave. It sounded strange since he was normally a cheerful person.

"That does sound logical. If they're willing to kill an innocent baby, it makes sense that they would try to do something like this," Ginger said. Her eyes were filled with sympathy, but her voice wasn't optimistic.

"You all think that the watchers planted this note so they'd be able to kill me eighteen years after their first attempt? That seems a little like overkill to me," I said.

"Extremists don't consider anything overkill," Ginger whispered.

"I found it!" Giselle exclaimed.

"Found what?" Rowan and I asked in unison.

"The address. It's a small brick house about two hours away from here. There's a pretty herb garden in the backyard. It doesn't seem like the type of thing that an evil, malicious person would have." Giselle smiled at me. She didn't appear to be worried.

Rowan sighed. "Fine. It's Lily's decision."

"There's a chance that going to this house might help me find my mother, so I'm going to go. But that doesn't mean that any of you have to go with me. I know it could be dangerous, and I won't subject any of you to that unwillingly." I looked at each of them, attempting to read their facial expressions.

"Lily, we're going with you. What else are friends for if not to follow you into potentially life threatening situations?" Ginger grinned.

"This time we'll be prepared. Each of us is going to be carrying weapons, just in case," Rowan said.

"Oh yes, to battle the evil, herb garden-growing villains," Giselle laughed.

Rowan rolled his eyes. "We'll go on Saturday."

I truly had the most wonderful friends in the entire world.

Chapter 23
To Grandmother's House We Go

On Saturday morning Ginger, Giselle, Rowan, and I drove to the mystery address. My parents had left the house before I even woke up and wouldn't be home until late, so I didn't need to explain to them why I'd be gone. Rowan was adamant that he was going to drive, so we took his car. Ginger and Giselle sat in the backseat, and I sat in the front next to Rowan. Rowan was insistent that each of us carried small knives in our pockets, along with pepper spray. Giselle had argued with him for around ten minutes, saying that if we walked into my mom's house with knives and pepper spray she might be slightly offended. Rowan refused to compromise, so eventually she gave up.

We arrived at the house around noon and parked along the street a few houses away. Rowan said that we didn't want to park too close to the house because we didn't want them to know we were coming. Giselle rolled her eyes at this, muttering something about how we were being rude guests. Ginger was silent most of the time, clutching her knife and pepper spray as if her life depended on it. I tucked both my knife and pepper spray into my purse, hoping that I wouldn't need them.

We walked down the sidewalk and up the driveway. Rowan, who was walking considerably faster than the rest of us, reached the door first. The house looked exactly as Giselle had described. It was a small brick house with lots of green hanging plants on the front porch. It didn't exactly look like the home of a stereotypical murderer.

Giselle was humming a happy tune. Rowan frowned at her and knocked on the door. After he'd turned away from her, Giselle stuck her tongue out at him. Ginger sighed while I tried to hide my smile. It was a nervous smile, but I was glad to be able to have any type at the moment.

The door started to slowly open, and I saw both Ginger and Rowan reach for their knives. Giselle was smiling brightly, as if she was about to see a long-lost friend. Not knowing what to do, I just stood still.

A small, grey-haired old woman opened the door, frowning slightly. She had piercing blue eyes, blue eyes that I remembered from the pictures of my mother. Rowan, who had turned red with embarrassment, quickly slid his knife into his back pocket. She looked at Rowan first, then at Ginger and Giselle. Finally, her eyes landed on me. Her face immediately registered shock, which quickly turned to disbelief.

"Come in," she said, holding the door open. She moved back into the hallway, letting Rowan hold the door for us all to walk inside.

Behind me I heard Giselle whisper, "I told you so!"

The woman led us into a small sitting room with furniture that looked to be around thirty years old. There were two large, orange Persian cats sitting on the couch. They watched us as we walked in, one of them hissing in Rowan's direction.

"Sit," the woman said, walking out of the room.

Giselle sat down beside the cat that had hissed at Rowan. She stroked its fur as it began to purr. Ginger sat down beside her, smiling. Any fears she might have held had obviously been dissolved. Rowan and I sat down in two armchairs across from Ginger and Giselle. Rowan's face was still bright red with embarrassment. Giselle was smirking, obviously pleased with herself. Ginger looked relaxed for the first time all day. I couldn't manage to get my mind off how eerily similar the old woman's eyes had been to my mother's. She was much too old to be my mother, who was only forty, but she was around the age my grandmother would have been.

We sat in silence until she returned, carrying a tray full of sandwiches and cookies. She set the tray down on the coffee table in the middle of the room. Walking over toward the window, she sat in a rocking chair, folding her hands in her lap. Her long grey hair was pulled up into a high bun with small flower pins sticking out of it. Mechanically, I reached up to touch my flower pendant hanging around my neck. It seemed that flowers were a common decorative symbol worn by faeries. The room was deathly quiet, other than the sound of Giselle happily chewing and stroking the cats.

"I knew it was you the moment I saw you. You look exactly like your mother, except for your eyes of course." The woman smiled slightly.

"You're my grandmother, aren't you?" I asked.

She smiled brighter this time. "I see you have your mother's intelligence. Yes, I'm your grandmother. I'm also the one who placed the note with this address on it in the box your mother left for you."

"Why didn't she leave it herself?" I asked.

"She thought that any future connection to us would only endanger you further. I never wanted her to give you up, you see. I even offered to raise you myself, using the excuse that you were an abandoned faerie child who needed a home. But she thought you were safer in a human family. However, I see that you've already found your way into the faerie community that Jane wrote about in her letter. I insisted that she include that detail. I knew you would need to be around faeries once you were older. May I ask you who you all are?" She gestured to Ginger, Giselle, and Rowan.

"Of course, ma'am. My name is Rowan Marx. I'm Lily's boyfriend." Rowan smiled at her.

She smiled back at him. "It's lovely to meet you, Rowan. My name is Clare."

Giselle grinned at her. "I'm Giselle, and this is my sister, Ginger. We're Rowan's cousins—"

"And Lily's best friends," Ginger cut in.

Clare looked amused. "I'm glad to know that Lily has such outgoing friends. If she's anything like her mother, she probably keeps to herself most of the time."

I blushed heavily.

"She's exactly like that," Giselle said as she reached for another cookie. Both cats protested, angry that she had stopped petting them.

"I see," Clare said, smirking.

I shot an evil glare at Giselle, who didn't appear to notice.

Clare saw the silent interaction and chuckled lightly. "Yes, exactly like her mother."

Rowan grinned at me, but stopped when I sent him the same look I'd given Giselle.

"If you don't mind my asking, where is my mother now? We came here with the intention of finding her." I looked directly at Clare, pleading with her to give me an answer.

Clare sighed, all of the previous amusement draining from her face. "I knew you would ask that. I tried to tell Jane that once you knew, you would try to find her. She told me that no one would ever search for a mother they never knew, especially not one who had abandoned them."

Ginger and Giselle were both staring at the ground, obviously depressed by her comments. Rowan reached for my hand, holding it protectively.

Clare walked over to a bookshelf in the corner of the room. "These were your mother's books."

I looked at some titles on the shelf, examining them. I took a deep, involuntary breath when I saw both *Sense and Sensibility* and *Wuthering Heights* side-by-side on the top shelf. Rowan followed my gaze, and after seeing the titles, squeezed my hand. I smiled at him, trying to avoid becoming overly emotional. I was here to find my mother, not to cry about her.

Clare gently took a picture frame off the middle shelf and brought it over to me. She handed me the photo, gazing at it longingly. I immediately recognized my mother. She was standing in the middle of the picture holding a small boy who looked similar to both her and me. In front of her were two other boys who looked a few years older than the youngest one. Kissing her cheek was a tall, dark-haired man. He was bulky with broad shoulders and extremely defined muscles all over his body. The two older boys looked more similar to him than my mother. They were all smiling happily in the picture.

"That's Chris; he's a water faerie. He married your mother ten years ago," Clare said, sensing my discomfort.

"Does he know about me?" I asked nervously.

Clara smiled triumphantly. "Yes. In fact, he's urged Jane to search for you ever since she told him. A man after my own heart."

I looked back down at the picture. My mother had not lost her beauty with age. She could have easily been mistaken for my older sister rather than my mother. But the innocence that had been in her eyes in the pregnancy photos was not present in this one. She looked more worldly, and some might even say sad. She was smiling, but there was an element of loneliness in her eyes.

I felt Clare put her hand on my shoulder. "She never stopped loving you, child."

"Where is she?" I asked, trying to control the emotion in my voice.

"They live on the Gulf Coast. After you were born, she wanted to leave the area. They bring the boys here to visit for about a week three times a year." Clare gently stroked my hair.

It was comforting, the type of thing you'd expect a grandmother to do.

"I'm going to find her even if she doesn't want me to," I said, handing the picture back to Clare.

"I know that. It's exactly what she would have done," Clare said, smiling sadly at me.

She took a small piece of paper out of her pocket and handed it to me. It was on the same type of paper that the note with her address had been on. This one had another address on it, my mother's. She was in Louisiana.

"Thank you," I whispered.

She reached down and hugged me. "After eighteen years, it's the least I can do."

She put the picture frame back on the bookshelf and picked up a small box that had been sitting beside it. She brought the box over and handed it to me. Like the box that had contained the letter from my mother, this box was also hand-painted. It was black and covered in small, golden flowers. On the top of the box the letters J and J were intertwined with the unity symbol painted in silver.

"I want you to have these," she said.

I opened the box to find three silver rings on a golden chain. They were my parent's wedding rings, along with my mother's engagement ring.

"Are you sure?" I asked.

"Completely. Jane gave them to me after she remarried. She told me to keep them safe, but I think that's your responsibility now." Clare smiled at me.

"Thank you, Clare." I smiled at her.

"Call me Grandma," she said, brushing a stand of hair out of my face.

I gently closed the box, putting both it and the note with my mother's address on it in my purse.

"We should probably be going. We have a long drive back," I said.

Ginger and Giselle, who had both been crying, quickly wiped the tears out of their eyes, and smiled. They stood up. Giselle said goodbye to the cats, promising them that she'd be back. Rowan walked over to me, lacing his fingers through mine.

I hugged Clare. "I'll come back soon, Grandma."

She smiled at me. Ginger and Giselle went outside first, leaving Rowan and me with Clare.

"Take care of my granddaughter," she said.

"I will." He kissed her lightly on the cheek.

She smiled at both of us as we walked out the front door waving goodbye.

Rowan put his arm around me as we walked to meet Ginger and Giselle near the car. He knew me well enough to know that I didn't want to talk, that I just needed to be held. He put both of his arms around me and kissed me. I pulled away, looking back at the house one last time before getting in the car. I saw Clare looking at us through the window. She winked at me before walking away.

Chapter 24
Will You....

Sunday afternoon Rowan and I walked into the meadow. After the stressful events of the previous day, I just wanted to be somewhere with Rowan where I knew we wouldn't be bothered. The meadow was as calm and peaceful as usual. Since it was almost summer, there were even more wildflowers than there had been the last time I was there. I heard a soft chirping sound and looked up. There in the apple tree beside me was a bird's nest, with three baby birds impatiently waiting to be fed. They continued to chirp for several more seconds before their mother brought them a couple of worms to share.

"There's something I want to show you." Rowan took my hand, leading me toward the lake.

"What is it?" I asked.

We stood in front of the lake looking down into the water. Rowan directed a beam of sunlight so that I could see the bottom more clearly. There was a large, smooth stone at the bottom with an engraving on it. I bent down to get a better look. It read, *Jack & Lily – Part of my heart will forever be with you*. I felt the tears run down my cheek and reached up to wipe them away. But before I could, Rowan's hand was already there, wiping the tears away with his thumb. He pulled me toward him and held me in his arms. I buried my face in his chest, breathing in his familiar scent.

"I know how much he meant to you," he whispered.

"How much he'll always mean to me," I replied.

"I know," he said.

"Thank you," I mumbled.

"Anything for you," he replied.

I leaned up and kissed him. I knew that he could taste the tears on my lips, but he didn't seem to care.

We were sitting on the grass staring at the lake when Rowan broke the silence.

"There's something I meant to ask you today." He moved his arm from behind my back and reached into his pocket. "I know that people usually wait longer than a couple of months after meeting each other, but I can't waste any more of the precious time I have with you, being apart." He knelt on one knee, holding a small black box in his hand. "Since the day I met you, I realized there was no other girl in the world like you. You're intelligent, kind, and loving. You're even funny, though you don't usually intend to be. You love books just as much as I do, which is something I thought I'd never find in a girl. You're beautiful; I know that you don't see it, but I do. You don't care what society or culture say you should be like. You're just yourself all the time, and I love that about you. But that's not all. There's so much more to us than simple personality traits. Even if you were none of the things I just said I loved about you, I'd still want to be with you. Our love goes so much deeper. I am just as much a part of you as you are of yourself. To lose you would be to lose the best, most innate part of who I am. I'm not just a part of you, I'm completely and wholly you. I am you the same way that you are me. To live without you, no matter how much more peaceful my life might be, would be to live without life itself.

I don't know if soul mates are real, but I do know that your soul and mine are two identical halves of one whole. So, Lily Rhodes, will you do me the honor of becoming my wife?"

His eyes seemed to burn through mine with an intensity that could have made mountains move. I hadn't expected him to ask this question, at least not for several more years. Don't get me wrong, I wasn't disappointed. Like any girl, I wanted this more than anything. Who didn't want to be swept away by their prince? I'd give up everything in the world to be with him.

"Yes," I whispered.

He opened the box to reveal a small silver ring with tiny diamonds embedded in it the whole way around.

"This was my mother's engagement ring. I know you probably want to get married with your parents' rings, but I thought this would do for now." He slipped it on my ring finger, his hands shaking.

I'd never seen his hands shake from nervousness before. I gently placed my hand on top of his, causing him to stop shaking.

"I love you so much." He untucked a strand of hair from behind my ear, letting it fall softly on the side of my face.

"Not as much as I love you," I whispered, reaching up to pull his face toward mine.

Chapter 25
LETTERS TO SEND

Graduation wasn't a particularly complicated affair. As valedictorian, I gave a short, hopefully memorable, speech about the benefits of being a life-long reader. Despite my assurance that reading was what had made me successful, most of the students simply rolled their eyes, ignoring the entire thing. It was their loss, not mine. If they wanted to spend their whole lives being "entertained" by some dumb sport rather than enjoying a good book, they were only hurting themselves. Well, also all the other people that were forced to interact with them, but mostly just themselves. I couldn't fix all the world's problems with one speech.

Of course, Rowan paid attention the entire time. Besides my parents and a couple of teachers, he was the only one to stand up and applaud at the end.

Several college recruiters came up to me after graduation and offered scholarships, sometimes even full-rides, if I wanted to attend. They were good colleges, too; Harvard, Brown, and Boston University were my best offers. But since Rowan and I were getting married in a couple of months, we'd decided that neither of us would go away to college. We'd already both been accepted to online colleges, where I'd be studying business and he'd be studying English literature. I planned on helping my parents run the bookstore until they retired, when I'd have to run it by myself. Rowan was going to help me with the store, but he also wanted to start a blog reviewing the twelve most popular books of each year. Until we started working, we were going to live off the money his parents had left, of which there was plenty.

It was three weeks after graduation, and I was still receiving more college mail. I took them off the pile on the table and put them in one of the many boxes I was packing. This box was dedicated to high school mementoes. To say the least, it wasn't a very big box. It contained mostly pictures and the dozens of scholarship offers I'd received in the mail. I thought they were worth keeping, if only to remember that I'd been able to earn them.

I shut the box, taping it up securely. I was attempting to pack several boxes a day so that I wouldn't have to worry about wedding events and packing at the same time. It sounded extreme, but we'd already delivered seven boxes full of books to Rowan's house. He'd offered to unpack them for me, but there wasn't enough space for them on the shelves. He had five bookshelves, but they were already double stacked and couldn't hold any more. So he'd ordered several more shelves to put in one of the spare bedrooms. I put the high school memento box on top of the ever-growing stack of boxes inside my bedroom.

It was hard to find a way to escape from Ginger and Giselle. They were in charge of planning the wedding, but seemed to ask my opinion on even the most trivial things. I couldn't tell the difference between Earl-grey napkins and French-grey napkins. Chances were, even if I could tell them apart, I probably wouldn't have cared which one was selected as the color of the tablecloths. I intended to spend my time at the table eating, not examining the decorations.

But right now, I seemed to have a moment to myself. I sat on my bed surrounded by dozens of boxes and prepared to start a letter that I'd been avoiding writing for over a month. I took out my box of stationary and selected several sheets of cream colored paper with small red roses around the edges. I picked up a fancy-looking black pen and began to write.

Dear Jane,

This is probably the strangest letter I've ever written. I only found out about a month ago that you're my mother. I didn't even know I was adopted until I discovered my abilities. My adoptive parents told me soon after that I was adopted at birth. They gave me the box you left for me, and I read your letter. I also met your mom, Clare. She was very helpful, and gave me this address so that I could write to you. It took me a while to find the courage to write this letter, but I knew it had to be done. So, just as you wrote a story for me to read in the letter you left for me, I now have to write one for you to read.

I was entirely oblivious to the world of fae until several months ago. I met a faerie, Rowan Marx, who I soon became friends with. I discovered that he was a faerie, and we quickly became more than friends. He lives in the community of faeries you wrote to me about, though his parents are dead. Coincidently, Forest Jones, the man you mentioned in your letter, is his uncle. Strangely enough, Forest's daughters, Ginger and Giselle, have become my best friends. They have a very close-knit family group, and are all very friendly. They were accepting of me even when everyone thought I was human. I'm sure you would like them.

Unfortunately, we had an incident with a few watchers. My best friend, who I'd thought was human, turned out to be from a family of watchers. Thinking that I was a human having a relationship with a faerie, his parents gave him the task of killing me. Before he had a chance to try this, Rowan's psychotic ex-girlfriend, Delilah, offered to help him. She wasn't from a family of watchers, but she wanted to kill me because she was jealous. She was convinced that she had some claim to Rowan that I was violating. They attempted to kill me, but obviously it didn't work. Rowan and some others came to rescue me before they did much damage. I did get a chance to stab Delilah in the shoulder before she got away, which is very satisfying to look back on. During the fight, I ended up discovering my powers and used them to defend myself. The rest of it is pretty self-explanatory.

There are a few reasons that I knew that I had to write this letter. The first is that I wanted you to know is I don't blame you for anything. I think what you did, giving me up, was incredibly brave. I don't know if I could ever have as much courage as you did. Not only do I forgive you for letting me go, but I'm so grateful for the thoughtfulness with which you selected my adoptive parents. They have been good to me, and gave me a perfect childhood. Because of where you placed me, I was also able to meet Rowan, Ginger, Giselle, and all of the other faeries that have come to play an extremely important role in my life. So thank you for giving me the chance to live a happy life, even though it wasn't with you.

The next reason I'm writing this letter is that I truly want to meet you. I want to be able to talk to you and to show you who I've become. If you're willing, I'd love for you to be a part of my life.

The last reason for this letter is also the most selfish. Rowan and I are getting married on August fifteenth. I'd love for you to be there. I'm inviting Clare as well, so I hope you'll come. I want my mom to be at my wedding. Even if it's the only time I ever see you, I'd really appreciate it if you came.

I hope that this letter makes you happy knowing that the

baby girl you gave up eighteen years ago has a life full of joy and love. Clare showed me a picture of your family; it's beautiful. All three of your boys are as handsome as their father. One day, maybe after we've had a chance to talk, I'd like to meet all of them too.

Your daughter, Lily Rhodes

PS: I thought that you'd like to know that your guess was right. I am an Earth faerie, just like you.

I set the letter down, examining it one last time. I didn't want her to feel obligated to come, not if she didn't want to. But I really did want her to come. Maybe she'd want to come too, but I doubted it. After eighteen years, how much could she really care? She had a new family now, a husband who wasn't my dad, and three beautiful children. She wasn't lacking anything, so why would she need me? She didn't need me, but maybe she'd want me. That was all that I could hope for. And really, it was better this way. If she came it would be because she wanted to, not because she felt that she had to.

I folded up the letter and put it inside an envelope, adding a wedding invitation along with a picture of Rowan and I. It was one of the pictures where we were looking into each other's eyes smiling. I chose it because it looked very similar to one of the pictures of my mom and dad that I had in my box. I thought that maybe she'd see the similarity and be compelled to come. I sealed the envelope and set it off to the side.

I started on another letter, this time to Clare. I had to remember to call her Grandma since she'd told me to.

Grandma,

I used the address you gave me and wrote a letter to Mom. I'm sorry I haven't visited since the first time we came to see you, but I really have been busy. Rowan proposed, so I've been trying to organize the wedding along with graduating. Of course you're invited to the wedding. It's August fifteenth. I invited Mom, too. If you can, please encourage her to come. It means a lot to me. Ginger and Giselle insisted that I tell you the wedding theme colors are grey and purple. I'm not sure why that's so important, but they were convinced that you'd want to know.

See you at the wedding,

Lily

Somehow, that letter had been so much easier to write. I knew she'd come to the wedding. She'd already made it clear that she was going to treat me like a normal grandchild. It was nice, since I'd never had any grandparents before. They'd all died before I was born — or rather, adopted. I took both letters downstairs and carried them outside to the mailbox. As I placed them inside, I took one last look at the letters, knowing they might provide the only chance I'd ever have to see my mom.

***

It had been a month since I'd sent the letters, and every day except Sunday I'd frantically searched through the mail hoping for a reply. I hadn't received one yet. Still I looked.

I went downstairs for my daily mail search, looking for any letters addressed to me. As usual, there weren't any.

Normally a bride would receive letters and bills having to do with her wedding, but Ginger and Giselle had taken charge of the letters while Rowan had taken the bills. Apparently, they didn't want me to see some of the things they were buying or how much they were paying for them. At Rowan's insistence, we'd spent no less than a thousand on my wedding dress. I'd said it was far too much. On the other hand, Rowan said he'd be happier if I spent more. It was definitely going to be strange getting used to his alternative standards.

Thankfully, I'd convinced everyone that the wedding should not be held at a fancy venue, but rather outside. I'd thought that the backyard would do just fine, considering that it was plenty big enough for the total of about a hundred people that Rowan and I wanted to invite. Unfortunately, Giselle had declared herself in charge of the guest list, and invited three hundred people. I honestly had no idea where she'd found them. I definitely didn't have three hundred friends. Three, without the hundred, was a much more realistic number. I was also pretty sure that Rowan wasn't friends with that many people. For all I knew, Giselle was paying strangers to come to my wedding. It wouldn't have surprised me one bit. No matter who they were, they weren't all going to fit in my backyard. So the wedding was going to be held at a local park.

After going through the mail a second time, I finally put it down. I decided to give myself a moment to relax and picked up a watering can to take outside to water my plants. Opening the door, I saw a box sitting on the doorstep. Kneeling down, I attempted to inspect it. It was for me! In my rush, I practically threw the watering can down and grabbed the box, rushed into the living room, and started ripping the tape off. It was one of those boxes with extra strong tape, the kind that an atomic bomb couldn't break, so my short, stubby nails weren't doing any good against it. As fast as I could, I sprinted into the kitchen, almost running straight into my dad, who was carrying a cup of coffee along with a newspaper. He was entirely oblivious to the almost-collision, and seemed not to notice how I was frantically looking for a pair of scissors.

With a somewhat intense feeling of relief that I had finally found them, I ran back into the living room. In a sloppy, haphazard mess, I cut the tape off the box and looked inside. There was an object covered in layers of bubble wrap, along with a small card. The card said that it was from Clare, and that although she was coming to the ceremony, she wanted to send this as an early wedding present. It didn't mention anything about my mom. My heart sank. I'd desperately wanted a reply from my mom. At least I knew that Clare cared, even if my mom didn't. I picked up the item and carefully cut away the ridiculous amount of bubble wrap surrounding it. It was a beautiful hair pin shaped like a rose, accented with tiny rubies. It was beautiful. There was no other word for it except beautiful. I'd wear it on my wedding day, along with my flower pendant from Rowan. They would match perfectly.

Chapter 26
An Unexpected Visitor

Someone was frantically shaking my shoulders, "We're late, we're late!"

I groaned, pulling my arms over my eyes. It was way too early for this—plus, I didn't even know what I was late for. If it was a dentist appointment, I wouldn't have minded being late for the rest of eternity.

"Lily, get up!" I now recognized the voice as belonging to Giselle. Why was she waking me up? Whatever it was, it couldn't possibly be that important, if I couldn't remember it. I felt Giselle hit my face with a pillow as she shouted, "Get up, it's your wedding day!"

My wedding day? It was my wedding day and I had overslept! I jumped up off my bed and dashed into the bathroom.

From somewhere behind me I heard Ginger say, "Well, that sure got her moving."

I practically ripped my pajamas off and jumped into the shower. The water was scalding hot against my skin, but I didn't care. The stress of it all, combined with the extra stress of being late, removed almost all physical sensation from my body. I quickly washed my hair and threw on my robe.

I ran back into my bedroom and was subsequently bombarded with all sorts of products. Ginger was drying my hair while Giselle was handing me dozens of creams. There were so many! I didn't think I could possibly need all of them. One was for dry skin, another was for dark-circles, and on and on they went. I tried to apply them all correctly, but she was handing them to me faster than I could even open the bottles. I was pretty sure I'd accidentally put the one for my feet under my eyes and the one for my hands on my feet. Honestly, after the first five, I just started rubbing them on in random places.

Ginger finished drying my hair and started pulling the top half of it up into a bun. She wrapped it tightly in a circle and began pinning it tightly to my head. Giselle had finally run out of creams to give me, and had now moved on to making me choose what colors of eyeshadow I wanted. Apparently she didn't like my choices, because she used different colors than the ones I'd selected. Giselle applied my makeup while Ginger curled the lower half of my hair into tight barrel curls. By now I was used to having them fuss over me. I was able to wait, relatively patiently, until they were finished working on me.

As soon as they were finished, we rushed downstairs to quickly grab something to eat. Ginger and Giselle both ate several pieces of toast coated in butter. They ate hurriedly, obviously anxious to go back upstairs to get themselves ready. I, on the other hand, was not moving quickly. I was completely comfortable with the idea of marrying Rowan, but that didn't mean I wasn't nervous. Three hundred people were a lot to impress. With my luck, I might fall down the aisle instead of walking down it. That would be mortifying. My birth mother hadn't even bothered to answer my letter, much less come to my wedding. Although it bothered me, there was nothing I could do about it. I didn't see the point in worrying about something I couldn't change.

Ginger and Giselle finished eating and went back upstairs. I sat at the kitchen table drinking my coffee while trying to calm my nerves. I was still wearing my bathrobe, but was otherwise ready to go. My parents, the adoptive ones that is, had been up hours before us. As much as my mom said she wanted to help me get ready, she was preoccupied with the florist, who had apparently been giving her trouble with the bouquet. So they'd left the house early, hoping to resolve the problem.

I set my coffee cup in the sink and started to walk back upstairs. I was halfway up the stairs when I heard a loud pounding at the door. It was strange, since I wasn't expecting anyone. But I went to open the door anyway, thinking it might be a caterer, entertainer, or any of the large number of people that had been hired to help with the wedding.

I opened the door to see Clare standing in front of me wearing a long, flowing, light pink dress. Her grey hair fell down at her sides in soft, gentle curls. I doubted I would ever look as regal as she looked in that moment, especially at her age. She was just the type of person whose presence demanded attention. She probably could have ruled the world if she wanted to, without anyone complaining.

"Grandma, I was expecting to meet you at the park. What are you doing here?" I motioned for her to come inside, but she shook her head.

"I have a surprise for you." She smiled, gesturing to her car, which was parked in the driveway.

I gave her a questioning glance before looking at her car. I could hardly believe what I was seeing. A woman, who looked almost exactly as I imagined I would look in about twenty years, stepped out of the car. She was wearing a hot pink pencil skirt along with a long-sleeved grey blouse. I appreciated her shoes, which were simple grey flats. I could relate to people who were similarly physically incapable of wearing heels. Her hair, which was shockingly similar to mine, was pulled into a large Dutch braid that fell down to her waist. She walked toward me holding a small box in her hand. She stood beside Clare, smiling sadly while looking at me. I looked into her familiar blue eyes, the blue eyes that I knew belonged to my biological mother. She was my mom.

Remembering that I was standing outside in my bathrobe, I ushered them indoors. I closed the door behind me, leaning on it for support.

"Lily." My mom wrapped her arms around me, placing my head on her shoulder. I stayed there for only a second, relishing in her scent. As strange as it seemed, her perfume smelled almost familiar. It was comforting. I pulled away, not wanting to ruin my makeup.

"Mom," I whispered, staring at her in unbelief.

"I brought you something."

She handed me the box, which I quickly opened. There was a white wedding veil folded up inside.

"It was the one I wore when I married your father." She smiled at me.

"Thank you, thank you for coming." I buried my face in her shoulder, not caring if I messed up my makeup. This was the best wedding present I could have possibly asked for.

After introducing Ginger and Giselle to my mom, it was time to get dressed. The girls put on their bridesmaid dresses first, which were absolutely gorgeous. They were Grecian-style purple dresses accented with small silver sparkles. Of course, being Ginger and Giselle, they both wore pairs of silver stilettos with their dresses. I, obviously, did not. I'd convinced both of them that I'd probably kill myself walking down the aisle if they made me wear heels. So they mercifully let me wear a pair of simple white ballerina-flats.

My dress, however, was far more complicated. It was a large, princess style dress which was high-necked with long sleeves. The bottom half was accented with glittering sparkles, while the top half was covered in white lace. It was what I'd always imagined as my wedding dress. Ginger helped me lift it over my head while Giselle fastened the buttons in the back. I fastened the necklace Rowan had given me around my neck. Ginger used the rose hair pin that Clara had given me, attaching it to the veil and then clipping it in front of my bun. I looked at myself one last time in the mirror before walking out the door.

We arrived at the park, and I was quickly escorted into a tent that had been set up for me and all of the other women in the wedding party. I noticed that a similar tent had been set up for Rowan and all of the men. We waited inside until my dad came to tell us that it was time. Everyone else left first, giving me final smiles of encouragement. I smiled at my dad and held onto his arm as we walked down the aisle.

It had been wonderfully decorated. Purple flowers of all varieties spilled over the edges of large pots beside every row of chairs. Smiling faces watched me with excitement, some that I recognized and some that I didn't. Rowan stood at the end of the aisle under a large canopy, looking as breathtaking as ever. He smiled at me and winked.

When we finally reached the end, Ginger stepped up to take my bouquet, which was made up of purple and white roses. I took Rowan's hand, looking into his determined eyes. At that moment I was entirely certain about what to do.

After the ceremony I changed into a simple knee-length white dress. Rowan and I danced for about an hour before stopping to rest. We sat at our empty table, watching everyone else dance. Marie and Forest were dancing gracefully in the middle of the floor, attracting lots of attention. Ginger was dancing with her fiancé, who was much more down-to-earth than I'd expected him to be. My parents, all three of them, were standing in the corner of the dance floor talking. Clare was dancing with Carson right next to Athena, who was dancing with Cameron. Giselle was wandering around looking for something to drink. Rowan put his arm around me, and I leaned against his shoulder.

"I love you," he whispered.

"I love you, too," I said, placing my hand on his chest.

Everything was virtually perfect, but it didn't feel that way. There was something missing, something I'd been trying to forget since the day he walked out of my life. I'd tried not to think of Jack, and it had worked for a while, but not now. I'd always thought he would be there on my wedding day, supporting me through the whole thing. It just felt wrong, in a way I couldn't explain, for him not to be there. I had everything else I wanted: Rowan, my biological mom, and a honeymoon to look forward to, but not Jack. He was the only thing standing between me and absolute happiness. I knew what I had to do, but it would have to wait until after my wedding day.

Chapter 27
GOODBYE

It was the day after we'd gotten back from our honeymoon. Rowan and I had officially been married for almost two weeks now. We had enjoyed a beautiful week on the beach, visiting nice restaurants, and shopping. But now it was over. It was time to do what I'd known I had to do since the wedding reception. I slowly moved out from underneath the covers, attempting not to wake a still sleeping Rowan. Going into to the bathroom, I quickly changed into some casual clothes and braided my hair. I grabbed my shoes and a jacket and headed downstairs.

Moving through the various bookshelves, I finally found what I was looking for—my copy of *Dracula*. Jack had given it to me for Christmas our freshman year. I brought it to the kitchen table where I'd laid the rest of my supplies out the night before—a piece of cream colored cloth, a thin strip of leather, and a letter. With shaking hands, I placed the book on the cloth and wrapped it up, securing it with the strip of leather. As gently as I could, I slid the letter into my jacket pocket and zipped it up. I put the book in my bag and quietly walked out the front door, locking it behind me.

I walked up to where the entrance to the meadow was located and placed my hand on a large oak tree. It was the first time I'd been to the meadow by myself, but I'd become relatively comfortable with using my magic over the past few months, so I wasn't too worried. The rock in front of the path to the meadow was too heavy for me to move by myself. I willed the oak tree to help me and watched as one of its branches bent down, moving the rock just enough that I could walk through. I silently thanked the tree, patting my hand gently against it. I walked through the opening and over toward the lake.

My eyes began to water as I looked down at the rock at the bottom of the lake with my name and Jack's on it. Truthfully, I doubted that anyone except Rowan fully understood how important Jack had been to me, how important he still was to me. It was the type of bond that most people wished they could experience with a friend, but were rarely able to. I was grateful for the four years I'd been able to have with him, even though I'd miss him for the rest of my life. My heart ached and I hoped that wherever he was, he was content, maybe even happy. I was certain that he deserved to be loved. I couldn't believe that he was actually a bad person. The truth was that he was a good person who'd been forced to make all the wrong decisions. Honestly, he'd never really had a choice — or at least, he thought he'd never had a choice. The two were virtually the same thing. It killed me that he'd made himself a prisoner to his own perception of reality. Now he'd be forced to live in it forever.

I sat on the ground staring at the stone. Crossing my legs underneath me, I took the letter out of my pocket, preparing to talk to Jack for one last time.

Dear Jack,

I wanted to write you a letter telling you everything that's happened. We used to tell each other everything, or at least I thought we did. Now that I'm actually writing it, I can't seem to find any of the words I want to say. I'm married. I suppose that's the first thing I should tell you. I'm happy with him. I don't know if I could have made it after you were gone if he wasn't there. He's my rock, and I love him. You might have already figured this out since I used my powers for the first time on the day you left, but I'm a demi-fae. It's a long story, but the shortest way to explain it is that I'm adopted. My faerie mother gave me up after watchers killed my dad when she was pregnant. I've met my mom now, and we've decided to stay in touch.

    I was too harsh with you on the day you left. I'm sorry. I blamed you for all of it then, but now I see that you were just a pawn in their game. This whole thing is bigger than us, bigger than two kids who just want to be normal. It was never your fault, and I don't blame you. You can't stay mad at the people you love, and I love you. Not in a romantic way, but in a much purer version of love. I love you in a way that someone loves another who is their most trusted companion, the person they bear their soul to, because they know that they won't be rejected.

    I guess I probably won't ever see you again, but that's all right. You'll always have a little part of me with you wherever you go, and I'll have a little part of you. We've left marks on each other's souls that no amount of time can erase. The memory of you will always live in me, so I'll never really be alone. Thank you for showing me how beautiful life can be, how beautiful a true friendship can be. No matter where life takes you, you'll always be my Jack, my best friend.

    So here in the meadow, the place where all of our problems began, I'm making a memorial for you. It's simple, which is the way I think you would have wanted it. I'm leaving my copy of Dracula, the first present you ever gave me, beside the lake. I'm also leaving *this letter, because I know its words will find you in another way. Maybe in a hundred years, or two hundred, two of our descendants will meet. They could become friends or even fall in love. The universe seems to enjoy doing things like that, playing tricks on us mortals. I wish you happiness, Jack, all of the happiness in the world. I'll never forget you. I'll love you forever.*

> *As always, yours,*
> *Lily*

Feeling the tears roll softly down my cheeks, I folded the letter up and put it back in the envelope. With all the tenderness I could muster, I pressed my lips to it, placing a gentle kiss on the front where I had written his name. Softly I set the letter on top of the book and put both of my hands on the ground. Focusing my willpower, a small hole opened up where my hand had been touching the ground. My fingers traced the spine of the book as I set it, along with the letter, inside the hole. I began to cover them with dirt, but not before a few of my tears fell on the letter.

Having been so distracted, I didn't even realize that Rowan had walked up behind me. I hadn't told him where I was going this morning or what I was doing. He just knew me well enough to have figured it out. Rowan knelt down beside me, and placing his hand over mine, helped me completely cover it with dirt. He wrapped his right arm around me while taking a handful of seeds out of his pocket and softly pressing them into the dirt. Then he placed both my hand and his on top of them. Realizing what he was trying to do, I turned my focus toward the seeds. In a breathtaking moment, I felt the energy flowing out of my palm transferring to the seeds. My eyes grew wide in amazement as I saw the light flowing out from Rowan's hand. I could even feel how his energy helped lessen the strain on my own. The seeds started to grow and quickly became small plants, then blooming flowers. They were lilies, Martagon lilies. They're beautiful, but always look like they're crying. It was perfectly fitting.

I felt his arm tighten around me, pulling me closer. I let myself become enveloped in his embrace. He always knew exactly what I needed. It was the type of connection that only ever happened in books, in fairytales. This was it—this was my happily ever after.

Epilogue

I stood in the bathroom biting my nails, waiting for the most stressful two minutes of my life to pass. My hands were shaking with anticipation. I'd never thought that this moment would be stressful. I'd always imagined excitement, but never stress. Then I looked down. The two minutes were over, and there were two bright, clear, blue lines. I was pregnant.

I heard a shrieking sound piercing through the air. I had no idea what was causing it until I realized that it was coming from me. My hand mechanically flew up to cover my mouth as the sound stopped and the bathroom door flew open. Rowan looked at me, eyes wide and breathing heavily. His hair was a mess, his shirt was buttoned incorrectly, and there was a coffee stain on his pants.

"What happened?" he said, looking around the bathroom for anything that might have caused me to scream.

"I'm pregnant," I whispered, not taking my eyes off the test sitting in the sink.

"Huh?" He didn't seem to understand my words, or maybe he hadn't even heard what I'd said.

"I'm pregnant!" I shouted, a ridiculous looking smile creeping onto my face.

"You're pregnant? You're pregnant!" he shouted, picking me up off the floor. He spun me around, laughing, kissing me when he finally put me back on the floor.

One year later...

    It was dark in the nursery, but not as dark as it was outside. The two lamps in the corner of the room provided a soft glow that enabled a person to see. But they were not bright enough to eliminate the shadows on the faces of my tiny children. John, with his curly-blond hair and bright green eyes, was blissfully sleeping. He was not a light sleeper like his twin sister, but rather slept so soundly that he would not have woken if there were a hurricane raging outside the nursery widow. He had inherited that trait from Rowan. Mina, on the other hand, could never sleep more than three or so hours at a time. She was a fragile baby, much smaller and more easily upset than her brother. Her dark brown, silky hair and caramel colored eyes were another testament to just how different they were. Tonight, was one of the nights where she could hardly seem to sleep at all. She was a difficult baby, but we didn't mind.

    I stood in the nursery, gently rocking her as she drank some of my bottled breast milk. Her little finger wrapped around my hand as I held the bottle up against her mouth. My mouth crept into a smile as I heard Rowan's soft footsteps while he walked over to wrap his arms around my waist. A sigh escaped my mouth as I rested my head against his shoulder, leaning up to kiss his neck. My body relaxed into his as I felt his right arm tighten around me while he reached his left arm up to stroke Mina's hair. Truthfully, I'd never thought of myself as a person who would ever be completely content. Somehow, I'd always thought that I would constantly crave more out of life. But in that moment, my world was entirely perfect.

Abby Farnsworth is a teen author who enjoys sharing her creative energies with others through writing, singing, and acting. Her love of escaping into the fictional world of books led her to begin writing her own stories targeted at young adult and middle grade audiences. She enjoys traveling, cooking, yoga, British history, and sipping a cup of hot tea. Abby lives in WV with her parents, two sisters, and one brother. You can connect with Abby on Facebook at *www.facebook.com/ AbbyFarnsworth.Writer.Poet* where she shares updates on her current and upcoming projects.

Made in the USA
Middletown, DE
30 September 2021